# HEARTBEAT

Ever since her older sister jilted Paul Hume, Jenni Westcott has dreamed of being old enough to marry him herself. Now it seems her moment may have come . . . Jenni has arrived in Tanzania to work as a nurse at Paul's remote mission station. But nothing turns out as Jenni has planned. Paul is delighted to see her, but that is all — and Ross McDonnell, the Medical Officer in charge, is openly sceptical about her capabilities . . .

Books by Anna Ramsay
in the Linford Romance Library:

MISTLETOE MEDICINE

ANNA RAMSAY

# HEARTBEAT

*Complete and Unabridged*

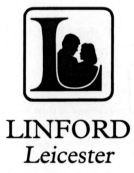

LINFORD
*Leicester*

First published in Great Britain in 1988

First Linford Edition
published 2014

A catalogue record for this book is available
from the British Library.

ISBN 978–1–4448–1795–9

Published by
F. A. Thorpe (Publishing)
Anstey, Leicestershire

Set by Words & Graphics Ltd.
Anstey, Leicestershire
Printed and bound in Great Britain by
T. J. International Ltd., Padstow, Cornwall

This book is printed on acid-free paper

# 1

She was aware of having been dumped unceremoniously on the treatment couch intended for patients. Through a haze of dizziness the young nurse sensed two men looming over her.

'The Sleeping Beauty!' joked one. 'Hey, man, if Ah kiss her Ah might turn into a prince. Whaddya think, doc?' The accent was definitely Dallas — which only added to Jenni's confusion.

A deeper voice, cynical and authoritative, with a faint twang of Down Under, crushed the American's enthusiasm with dry good humour.

'Shouldn't recommend it. You might turn into a frog.'

One solitary tear slipped from beneath Jenni's trembling eyelids and trailed down the side of her pale face on to the rough cotton pillowcase.

Somewhere above her head there was

an awkward silence. The two doctors exchanged glances.

Jenni's head was still going round and round and she dared not move for fear she might faint again. All she could do was trust to the charity of these two unsympathetic strangers, deep in the heart of the African bush.

★ ★ ★

After chilly London, the humidity of Dar-es-Salaam was proving a knockout, stifling and oppressive.

Every bone in Jennifer Westcott's slender body ached with weariness.

But supper at Mission Headquarters was clearly a sociable affair. The long refectory table was crowded with friendly faces, all eyes focused on the British nurse who had arrived late that afternoon. Nothing for it, sighed Jenni, but to keep the Westcott chin well up and make a mighty effort to look alert and interested. Even if I can't swallow a mouthful.

Sister Margaret, the redoubtable Scots nun who ran the domestic side, was ladling the steaming contents of a huge brown casserole on to white china plates. Heads were bowed and voices stilled as the good Sister said Grace.

Jenni inhaled the tangy aroma — and instantly her tastebuds sprang healthily awake! Mmm . . . fish simmered in some kind of vegetable sauce . . .

She sampled a forkful, and a beam of a smile spread over her expressive features. 'This is *delicious*! To think I was warned African food could be — er — '

She'd been about to say tasteless, but an imposing black headmaster was seated on her left and just in the nick of time Jenni transformed a potentially tactless remark into a convincing fit of coughing.

Sister Margaret found herself warming to this cheerful, uncomplaining newcomer. The redheaded lassie must be dog-tired in spite of putting a brave face on it, which augured well for the demanding job that lay ahead. 'Enjoy!' she encouraged. 'You won't get much fresh fish where you're going.'

Father Paul had spoken very highly of Jennifer Westcott and her vicarage family. And he had not been exaggerating, mused the shrewd nun, seeing for herself that this was a determined and intelligent young person. Only a girl of character would volunteer to work in the African bush. 'We use a local recipe called *samaki*, flavoured with lots of chopped frrresh coriander leaves,' she explained, rolling her rrs with relish as she ladled seconds on to Nurse Westcott's plate.

Och yes, just the sort we need out here, figured Sister Margaret; a lassie who won't hesitate to roll up her sleeves and get stuck in. As for that hair and those freckles — why, she'll take a bit of time getting acclimatised, but she'll be all right, this one. She smiled approvingly at Jenni's appetite. 'Ross McDonnell will be mighty glad to see you, m'dear. Puir man, he came to

4

Africa expecting to specialise in eye surgery — and found himself Dr Jack-of-all-trades!'

'I very much admire you British nurses,' murmured the dignified head-master, clearly taken with the freckled newcomer's cloud of coppery curls and her frank, open-featured face. 'You leave your homes and cross entire continents to help Africa and the Africans. I want you to know, Miss Westcott, that our joy and gratitude is deep and sublime because you offer your hearts to humankind.'

His sincerity was touching — Jenni felt her cheeks grow warm with a sense of shame. What would this grave African say if he knew the truth? That she had travelled here to offer her heart, not to humankind so much as to one very special man working deep in the Tanzanian bush.

Scalp itching in sympathy, she cast a rueful glance at Sister Margaret in her crisp blue veil, so cheerfully presiding over supper. Imagine having to wear

5

that thing all and every day in such sticky heat!

'With your colouring, Africa's the last place you should be going!' Mrs Westcott, the Vicar's wife, had sighed, knowing only too well that once her youngest daughter's mind was made up . . . 'You'll have to keep your head covered, darling, or you'll end up with sunstroke. And only pack clothes made from natural fibres.'

Mrs Westcott's electric Singer had whirred busily as she sewed for this six-month African venture, thankful that Paul, bless his heart, would be on hand to see the tempestuous Jenni came to no harm. Not that Jenni was a child exactly; not at twenty-four and a London-trained RGN.

On a nurse's salary a girl couldn't afford to splash out on a lot of new outfits to suit a tropical climate. Jenni too was a nifty dressmaker, but what with fitting in nutrition lectures at the London School of Hygiene and Tropical Medicine alongside her demanding job as staff nurse on one of the Royal Hanoverian's paediatric wards, she was very grateful for her mother's wizardry with Vogue patterns and colourful cottons chosen to complement Titian curls and freckled white skin.

It was *specially* important to look stunning for Paul.

If the parents — or her two married sisters, heaven forbid! — twigged what the youngest member of the family had in mind . . . why, they'd probably have a collective fit, the poor dears! Seduction (such a comical Victorian word) of sister Helen's ex-fiancé — now a missionary priest in the African bush. Well, the whole works: marriage, the gold band, *Mrs* Paul Hume . . .

This was why the African headmaster's generous words made Jenni bite her lip and lower protective lashes over eloquent golden eyes.

Of course she was distressed by the sufferings of his people; of course she wanted desperately to do her bit to help. But there was this other, very personal motive.

A trickle of sweat ran eerily down her spine.

Though it had started the evening looking daisy-fresh, the sleeveless apple-green dress with its easy dropped waistline and body-skimming fit was sticking uncomfortably to her shoulder-blades — even after the cool shower she'd gladly taken on arrival for this overnight stay. And everyone was being so kind, so friendly, so eager to help. The dry heat of the interior, they assured the newcomer, would prove much more tolerable: there, the nights would turn cool and even chilly. They hoped she had packed a sweater or two.

Jenni's sudden yawn would not have disgraced a hippopotamus.

'Ye puir wee creature!' crooned Sister Margaret. 'Gree-at black rings under y'r eyes. Away to your bed, child, you've an early start in the mornin'. So much travelling for a wee slip of a lassie, tch, tch!'

Sister glanced up at the big round

clock on the wall. 'Nine-thirty and *still* no sign of Dr McDonnell. Tch, tch, and he knew you'd be here today. That ma-an!'

Over supper Jenni had been told that Ross McDonnell, with whom she would be working out at the Good Shepherd Mission, was an eye surgeon from a big northern hospital back in the UK; one of a team of eye specialists recruited on temporary assignment by the World Health Organisation to tackle eye problems in the Third World. Dr McDonnell had signed up for nine months, with half his contract left to run. According to Sister Margaret, Ross was so acutely perturbed by the African predicament that he worked all the hours God sends — accounting for his typical lateness this particular evening.

Every three weeks or so the doctor would drive the long haul to Dar-es-Salaam to demonstrate complicated techniques in eye surgery to African doctors at the city's general hospital;

then he would collect fresh medical supplies for the mission station out in the wilds, and spend a couple of nights at headquarters, where Jenni was now en passant. Her arrival had fortunately coincided with one of his visits, saving the eager newcomer the discomfort of endless hours on the rickety local buses.

Jenni thought Ross McDonnell sounded a very nice and considerate and caring sort of doctor. He must be, to have volunteered for work such as this — and clearly in the nun's eyes he was the Archangel Gabriel and the Blessed St Luke rolled into one!

As for Father Paul — who while serving his curacy in her father's busy city parish had fallen in love and become engaged to the Vicar's eldest daughter — well! Judging by the conversation tonight *he* hadn't changed a bit. Handsome and athletic as a Greek hero, good-humoured as the day was long, loved by everyone he met . . . yes, that was Paul all right. Jenni's heart leapt in anticipation of the moment when she would set eyes on him again.

It was high time Paul came home and fixed himself up with a partner for life. Someone who would go with him to the ends of the earth — if that was what he was called to do.

★  ★  ★

Staff Nurse Jennifer Westcott, RGN, was a girl with a mission. She had promised herself at the tender age of seventeen, when Helen jilted Paul Hume — oh yes, it was a harsh word to use, but that was the truth of the matter — that she would one day marry him herself.

And now she was twenty-four. And in all her wide experience — for she was a pretty and lively girl with a host of admirers — a man to equal Paul had never materialised.

From the moment the aircraft had flown over the Equator, Jenni's excitement had spiralled with the plane's steady descent.

Somewhere down there Paul would be waiting. She hadn't seen him for almost eight years, not since she was a sixth-former planning a nursing career at the same London hospital where her sisters had both trained.

What would he think of her now? An assured and responsible twenty-four-year-old, far removed from the naïve little Jenni of vicarage days. Volunteering her professional skills for the work of the Good Shepherd Mission.

She peered into the cottonwool clouds as if to find Paul's darling face, haloed with cropped blond curls, grinning up from out of what seemed a giant lake of soapsuds.

The realisation that he hadn't after all come to the airport to meet her was a bit of a blow, but Jenni sensibly abandoned herself to the adventure of sorting things out for herself. She had been brought up to stand on her own two feet and was not inclined to be a worrier over trifles; all the same, when a beaming young African in a check

12

sports jacket introduced himself and said he'd been sent to escort her to Mission Headquarters, Jenni was quite pleased to find herself after all expected and provided for.

★ ★ ★

. . . Dark rings round the eyes sounded impressive evidence of fatigue. Even after a back-to-back shift of eight nights on duty she had never looked quite that interesting. After supper, in the privacy of her room Jenni went straight to the speckled piece of mirror above the stained china washbasin and peered at her face with concern. Two bright enough eyes stared back at her — surrounded by circles of melted brown mascara.

Jenni cursed her insipid eyelashes. She liked wearing make-up. And mascara was a basic essential when you bore the handicap of freckles and flaming hair.

'You look like a redheaded panda,'

she informed her image scornfully. 'Proper daft, as they'd say back home. You should have had your eyelashes dyed, like the others advised. Good thing you found out before you saw Paul. And your hair's going to be a problem. There's just — ' she dragged her fingers through the mass of bright curls — 'too much of it.'

Rooting in her case for cleansing cream and a cotton nightshirt before climbing into what looked like a baby's cot swathed in mosquito netting, Jenni turned up her folder of press cuttings, and was struck out of the blue by searing pangs of home-sickness.

For the past seven years the parishioners of Holy Trinity had held coffee mornings and car boot sales to raise money to send out to Father Paul and the Good Shepherd Mission. And when the local press heard that the Vicar's youngest daughter (all three girls were trained nurses) was going out to join Paul at the Mbusa Wa Bwino, there had been a flurry of interest and articles and photographs, which Jenni had carefully collected to show to Paul and everyone at the Mission.

She smoothed out the snippets of newsprint: not bothering with her glasses, for she could see the pictures well enough close to.

Herself, amidst a sea of familiar faces which included Dad and Mum, photographed on the church steps. Another of Jenni in nursing cape on a blustery winter's day, holding aloft the white flag with the familiar red cross, under the headline ANGEL OF MERCY FLIES TO THEIR AID. Then there were the packets of letters and photos sent by the children of Holy Trinity Junior School to the children of Paul's African parish.

Since there was no one to see, Jenni indulged in a little private sniffle which made her nose glow and her mascara run even more than it had already.

She had just begun to undress when heavy footsteps came purposefully along the corridor, and to her dismay

15

halted outside her very door. A demanding fist beat a tattoo on the wooden panel, and struggling back into her crumpled dress, Jenni called to her impatient visitor for goodness' sake to hold on for a moment.

Cautiously opening up, she discovered a filthy tramp, leaning threateningly with one hand on the door frame. She knew the nuns took care of such people and gave them food and shelter: but really, you wouldn't think they'd let them wander round the building disturbing genuine visitors. Hold on! said a warning voice in her head. This is Africa, and underneath all the muck, that's a white man.

A large and extremely dusty boot shoved itself deliberately across her threshold. The light in the passage was directly behind him, so that the face remained in shadow. He was very tall; she had to tip her head back to see him.

Jenni had the impression of a harshly lined face that couldn't have seen a razorblade for days on end. An

16

uncompromising head outlined in grey-ish stubble. And a pungent smell of heat and sweat emanating from the intruder's stained, crumpled and faded khaki fatigues.

She was not easily frightened. 'What do you want?' she demanded in her curtest tones. 'What can I do for you?' She wanted to take a step backwards and away from this threatening presence, but stood her ground.

The man's gaze had been levelled a good six inches higher, as if expecting the room to be occupied by a female Amazon. The girl's spirited question seemed to amuse him, and he smiled grimly: at least, his clamp of a mouth widened in some semblance of mirth. For a drawn-out moment he too stared back, with no sign that he liked what he was seeing any more than Jenni did.

'You're the nurse,' he said with rueful emphasis, drumming his fingers on the wooden door frame. 'Strewth!'

Even as she bridled at the clarity of the insult, Jenni was registering the twang of an Australian accent. She had a temper easily roused, but over the years she had learned to control it, tucking fists automatically clenched in anger under folded arms.

'I beg your pardon!' she snapped. 'I take it you are Dr McDonnell?' No way had he been operating, not in that condition. Not with that smell on his breath.

He didn't even bother to try to be polite. Already he'd seen as much as he wanted and lost interest, hooking his thumbs into his belt and turning to walk away.

'If you're not ready and out front by five-thirty, don't expect me to hang about.' The voice was curt, deep and well educated. The accent was slight; it must have been some years since he had quit his homeland for the UK.

'I shall be there.'

The shadowy head nodded, even as shrewd eyes noted that this slip of a kid was as whacked as Ross himself after that emergency call, coming at the end of a long and complicated day in theatre, to an outpost thirty miles distant.

'Oversleep, and you'll have to get yourself down to the bus station.'

'I told you, doctor, I shall be ready on time. Thank you,' she added, cool and over-polite, managing to shut the door exactly as he presented a long, lean and distastefully sweat-stained back: so that neither seemed to have the advantage of dismissing the other.

There was a stiffish key in the lock, and with a defiant wrench Jenni turned it, leaning for a moment with upturned palm pressed against solid wood while her breathing grew calm again and she considered the reality of Sister Margaret's *saintly* Ross McDonnell. Unwashed, unkempt, distinctly malodorous, and so arrogantly unconcerned with his physical appearance and the impression he was making on his new nurse that it was . . . well, it was insulting — that's what it was. Positively insulting!

It had never occurred to her that the Mission's doctor would find her unacceptable for some peculiar reason! Yes, she told herself, her heart racing with the shock of it; it was clear as the nose on her face that Dr McDonnell had not taken to his new nurse. Not at all. What a brilliant start to her stay in Africa!

Jenni chewed painfully on her bottom lip. She was not accustomed to being glowered at with blatant disapproval. Professionally she was both competent and capable, with certificates to prove it. And as a woman — well, men generally fell over themselves to be pleasant and attentive.

The confrontation had left her with a thudding heart and an uneasy sense that perhaps she had approached this African venture with high ideals and her head in a romantic cloud. Doubts assailed Jenni Westcott for the very first time.

But not for longer than a few brooding moments, for Jenni was an incorrigible optimist, and generous with it. The doctor was short-tempered and tired. She'd seen him in an uncharacteristic mood.

Yes, that was bound to be it. A cold shower and a decent night's sleep and the poor chap would be a different man by the light of day. No point getting upset over his attitude tonight. Besides — a mischievous smile transfigured the freckled heart-shaped face — she'd win him round. A dose or two of flirtatious charm and Dr McDonnell would be eating out of her hand — just like all the rest.

Sister Margaret's description of Dr McDonnell, though — a description so misleading as to make your hair stand on end! Tissueing away the last trace of mascara, Jenni did wish the bad-tempered doctor's first impression of her could have been a more positive one. Seeing his new nurse so drained and enervated by the damp heat, he'd be bound to assume she was pretty feeble. It would be a pleasure to show him otherwise! vowed Jenni with a gleam in her eye.

Curiosity lingered even after she was tucked up beneath the mosquito nets. She had been so preoccupied with the utter thrill of seeing Paul again that her professional relationship with the doctor at the Mission had simply not concerned her. In her mind's eye he had registered as an insubstantial and shadowy figure with whom she would . . . well, get on like a house on fire, as for the most part had been the case with her colleagues, nursing or medical, at the Royal Hanoverian.

★   ★   ★

'Where's Sister Margaret?' demanded Jenni.

'Sister is at early Mass. Perhaps I can help you?'

'Well, I do think McDonnell might have waited! I'm only forty minutes late.'

Persuaded to eat breakfast before being escorted to the teeming bus station, she winced to see her luggage casually heaved on to the dusty roof of a cream and orange bus which looked as if it might well disintegrate on the long drive westward into the interior.

'Oh, please do take care!' she called out to the African driver, as with lazy grace he tossed a heavy bundle on top of her cheap and shabby cases. Her own things didn't concern her, but the cases contained precious vaccines wadded round with towels to protect them from damage, medicines and plastic bags filled with powdered milk, all donated by Dad's parishioners back home.

Loose-limbed and bare-armed, the driver grinned confidently down at her and nodded his head, indicating that Jenni should get inside and grab herself a front seat.

At first the curious eyes and jabber of dialects among her fellow travellers was disconcerting, a child fingering the bright curls peeping out from beneath the blue scarf Jenni had tied gipsy-style to reduce the impact of her strangeness.

True to his word, the perfidious Dr McDonnell had not bothered to wait even an extra five minutes, but on the dot of five-thirty had driven off in a truck freshly loaded with medical supplies.

And all this stuff lugged out from the UK! grimaced Jenni, ruefully surveying her heap of belongings. McDonnell might at least have taken the two big cases on ahead, even if the Westcott company was unappealing.

The African day started bright and early. As the bus rattled through the city streets Jenni, from her vantage point, gazed down on the colourful throng, staring blatantly through dark lenses at the astonishing variety of people's attire: traditional African robes merging with casual Western clothes and cover-up Moslem dress. For the journey she herself had put on workmanlike dungarees in a frivolous rose pink, with a loose white T-shirt under the bibbed front. The early morning had been surprisingly pleasant and the outfit had seemed appropriate for travelling into the bush.

Relieved to be rid of its weight, she had dumped down her big canvas shoulderbag, ready to move the obstacle the instant anyone looked brave enough to sit beside her.

A plump black woman in a smart flowered dress clambered on to the bus with a basket full of long, green-whiskered heads of maize, a delightful baby Jenni judged to be about nine months old clamped to her left hip. Chattering in an unrecognisable local dialect — which sounded very much like mother and baby talk the world over — the plump woman settled in the seat in front, directly behind the driver.

The baby stared with unblinking liquid eyes and a mouth like a rosebud, claiming all Jenni's attention and quite distracting her from her annoyance with Ross McDonnell.

As the African landscape unfolded before her eyes Jenni was lost in the wonder and excitement of experiencing for herself the country that had been

Paul's home for the past seven years. In the far distance, outlined against a dark blue sky, stretched the purple outline of the Kilosa mountains. They seemed to the wide-eyed nurse to represent hopes and dreams at last becoming reality. The red of the African soil cheered her, the pastoral beauty of the countryside surprised and gladdened her heart. Oh, but she had been right to come.

The bus rattled along at a steady if monotonous twenty-eight miles an hour, grinding to a halt at dusty junctions near villages and settlements to disgorge noisy chattering passengers.

Fewer people were boarding now. Apart from the mother and babe in front, Jenni was surrounded by empty seats.

As time passed and the sun climbed higher, the baby lolled limp in the heat and the mother plied it with water from a plastic feeding bottle. Jenni wondered how far they were travelling. Perhaps they were from the village close by the Good Shepherd Mission; she regarded them with renewed interest and a quickened sense of responsibility.

Now, as they left the coast behind and penetrated ever deeper into the sparsely populated Tanzanian interior, the open landscape was becoming increasingly flat and arid. Everything was brown to Jenni's curious eyes. A landscape of tall brown elephant grasses studded with thorn bushes, and isolated baobab trees, their spongy bottle trunks bloated with conserved moisture. This mix of bush and grass and baobab trees, crossed by dried-out river beds, was the African bush. Here was the land in which Paul had chosen to spend seven long years, instead of the two he had originally planned for.

Jenni had believed he would return when she was twenty. But her sister Helen had married another man, and Paul had not come back.

The bus diverted from the tarmac highway on to impacted red dirt roads, travelling bumpily through a forested region. Progress became even slower as the roads deteriorated. Jenni's back began to ache with cramp and she explored dry lips with a tongue that felt swollen and parched. She wished she'd packed a map in her hand luggage, but had assumed the doctor would point out the route as they drove west.

Ross in his Land Rover must have reached the Mission hours before.

As her discomfort intensified, Jenni found it a distinct effort to feel charitable towards the inconsiderate Dr McDonnell. In an imperfect world there was bound to be a fly in any pot of ointment. Somehow she must suppress her increasing dislike of this man and seek to establish a working relationship, a *modus vivendi* that would make being thrown together bearable. In a small outpost mission disharmony would not be welcome; the last thing needed to complicate Paul's life and work.

The sun beat down upon her, burning her face and arms through the dusty window. The mother, clutching baby and basket, got off at the next village, and Jenni felt quite regretful to see them disappear from view.

Now she was the only passenger left. Hers must be the next stop.

The driver had promised to put her down near the Mbusa Wa Bwino Mission. It couldn't be long now — oh, please let it not be long now. And let Paul be there to meet her . . .

Jenni pulled off her headscarf and tried to fluff out the damp, squashed curls with nervously excited fingers.

Her stomach felt strange and queasy. How dreadful if she should throw up at his feet! How unromantic! Not that Paul would turn a hair. He would swing her up in his strongly muscled arms and carry her off to the peace and privacy of a cool shady room, his little Jenni, alone together at long last.

# 2

The solitary tear left a shiny trail down the freckled cheek.

A masculine throat cleared itself. The deeper voice spoke again.

'Go and make yourself useful. Unload the rest of those supplies before they take a walk.'

'Spoilsport!' complained the Southern drawl. 'Where d'you wannem, boss, the dispensary?'

'Uhuh. Get some of the boys to help you.'

'Right on, boss.'

There was a sigh. 'Don't keep calling me boss.'

'OK . . . Dr Ross.'

'Clear off, Matt, will you?'

There was a click of obedient heels — and now just the one black silhouette outlined against the intense daylight streaming in through a small high window, leaning over the treatment couch.

Ross McDonnell stared dispassionately down at his new nurse. Skin freckled like the inside of a foxglove petal. God help this one under the African sun — she'd fry like a chip!

The thrust of lower lip gave his face a formidable expression that discouraged argument. Ross was not a man to suffer fools gladly. And he'd got a right idiot here under his nose.

Vexed, he ran a hand across the stubble of his shorn hair. Take a look at the silly creature now. A fleeting taste of the hot stuff and she'd collapsed in a heap *inches* from the squealing wheels of the Red Cross Land Rover. She'd been lucky not to be killed, standing there lost in the cloud of red dust. Now if Matt had been driving . . .

Dammit, what could Paul be thinking of, encouraging this wide-eyed milkmaid to come tripping out here to do her dainty bit for the Third World?

You could see, mused the doctor

with folded arms and heavy-lidded scrutiny, that the journey had turned out an ordeal for such a fragile flower, even though he'd left her to sleep in as long as she needed. Well, his mind was made up. A fragile flower would never flourish in scorched earth; she'd be no earthly good to him. Once this young woman was rested she'd best turn her remarkably pretty self about and get back to darkest Sheffield, or wherever it was she'd come from.

Yes indeed, decided Ross, scanning the dirty pink dungarees and the damp golden eyelashes. No room for lame ducks here at the Mission. Paul's 'little sister' or no, the lady must return whence she came. 'Little sister, my foot!' scowled the disbelieving doctor. 'This one's no little *sister*. More like Trouble with a capital T.'

He chivvied her with brusque impatience, 'Wake up, milkmaid, some of us around here have got work to do!'

The closed eyes snapped open, an

unusual golden-hazel tinged with alarm. They latched on to the stethoscope around the doctor's neck.

The girl sat bolt upright. 'You're not examining me!' The eyes flashed a clear amber warning. 'I'm perfectly all right,' she continued spiritedly. 'You don't suppose I normally carry on like a Victorian miss in a laced corset, do you?'

Ross glanced at the white knuckles gripping the straps of the dishevelled pink dungarees — for all the world as if she expected him to tear her clothes off given the least encouragement. He bared his teeth in a grin.

'No need for a more intimate examination . . . this time,' he added, deliberately provoking another flash of warning amber. The first good-looking woman to come his way in weeks. Pity she must be got rid of; but he hadn't come to Tanzania to play games, however spirited the opposition.

And you don't look any cleaner today, Dr McDonnell! noted Jenni in disgust, not yet realising that her undignified nosedive into the road had taken its toll of her own appearance. Warily she gave him the once-over.

Aggressive stance deliberately assumed to intimidate the female. Ah yes! typical of an irritating breed of doctor — apologies, *surgeon* — who grabs the least opportunity to exert authority over the nurse-handmaiden. Arms folded to emphasise the strongly developed biceps and superior strength of the brute. Bold eyes in a suntanned face; grey eyes; astute eyes, splintered with the ice of dislike.

'I've made an enemy!' Jenni told herself with a sense of foreboding. 'I didn't imagine it. He's looking down his nose at me as if I'd crawled out from under a stone. Well, whatever I'm supposed to have done, Dr McDonnell, you ain't seen nothing yet!'

She returned his insolent stare with chin held high to conceal a desolate sense of loneliness. To come all this way and be greeted with such hostility . . .

But why? . . . And oh dear, *where* was Paul?

Ross had changed into khaki shorts, but the bush shirt looked like the one he'd been wearing last night — ugh! And every tough hairy inch of leg above the rolled-down wool socks and the heavy laced boots was filmed with the inescapable African dust.

She had thought that stubble on his head was grey, but she had been mistaken. It must have been dust. In daylight it showed up as a close-cropped lightish brown, almost the same colour as the tanned skin of his face and body.

Jenni looked down and saw the mess she herself was in, and her confidence wavered.

'I don't know what facilities you have out here, but I'd be grateful for a bath.'

'A *bath?*' came the derisive response. 'Out here we've neither the time nor the water for *baths*.' And time was too precious to waste more of it on this foolish creature and her selfish concerns.

'Where's Paul? He'll want to know I've arrived,' she said with chill dignity.

'I daresay. But work doesn't grind to a halt for every newcomer. Paul Hume does a lot of travelling. He'll be back this evening for our communal supper.'

'Can you — can you show me around the Mission?'

'Ask Dr Blamey, the guy who picked you up and carted you in here.'

Jenni slid her legs over the edge of the high couch and dropped to the floor, which was covered with tacked-down coir matting. She expected Ross to take a step back as she invaded his space, but he didn't move. Interesting.

Glancing up at the tall dusty doctor from under her lashes, Jenni murmured, 'Ah yes, the frog prince.'

There was a moment's pause. Ross McDonnell half-smiled.

The effect, accompanied by the slow regard of those heavy-lidded eyes, was disconcerting. Jenni's heart skipped a beat. Foolish heart.

She pulled a crumpled tissue from her pocket and rubbed spit into the dirty scratch on her upper arm, her imagination racing . . . Ross McDonnell was simply not her type. Not at all the handsome charmer she saw as her pre-ordained match. But his dismissive arrogance was a challenge, and he was excitingly different from the smoothies of the London teaching hospitals.

'Wait here.' Ross jiggled the keys of the Land Rover as he paused to look back at her from the doorway. 'Matt Blamey will show you the staff quarters. But be a sensible girl, right?' There was a patronising note to his voice that should have warned Jenni to be on her guard. But she was preoccupied with her own confused emotions.

'Don't bother to unpack. Just the stuff you'll need for tonight.'

'Wha — but I don't understand . . . '

'I'm going to drive you back to Dar-es-Salaam first thing in the morning.'

At the girl's sharp intake of breath his hand shot up, palm face outward in warning. 'I mean what I say. We've a strong chain of personnel here with no weak links. You're not up to it, milkmaid. I'm putting in a firm recommendation for sending you home. Tomorrow. Right?'

'Hold on a minute! Who do you think you are? You — you — ' Jenni spluttered in outrage; there wasn't a bad enough word in her vocabulary to describe the horrible man gazing down upon her as if she were some agitated beetle he was considering putting his boot on.

Another man materialised behind Dr McDonnell. A pair of interested eyes peered over his shoulder. 'I fetched some goat's milk — thought it might do her good.'

'Keep an eye on her, Matt. Bit overwrought — you know how it is.'

'Right on, boss.'

Speechless, Jenni gripped the edge of the treatment couch. A less spirited girl might have burst into tears. Her nails dug into the coarse sheet and her head spun with hunger and fatigue. But she was conscious that Matt Blamey was eyeing her in the way she had come to expect from men. He was going to be rooting for her, despite the hostility of this 'boss' man. Anyway, wasn't Paul the boss around here? What authority did Ross McDonnell have?

Well, he *is* the Medical Officer, and you are supposed to be working under his guidance, warned the voice of common sense. If McDonnell won't keep you, then I don't suppose he can actually make you leave the country; you'd have to transfer to another mission station where they were short-staffed.

Ross was gone. The atmosphere in the room lost its charge of electricity.

Over his jeans and red tartan shirt, Matt was now wearing a white doctor's coat with the collar carefully turned up — obviously a vital part of his image. And he had exchanged his sneakers for high-heeled cowboy boots. They looked hot and uncomfortable, but Matt didn't seem unduly bothered. Even in the boots he was several inches shorter than Ross McDonnell; but well proportioned on a lesser scale, slim-hipped and broad-shouldered, with smooth olive-toned skin. Matt's face, beneath the thatch of unruly black hair, was pleasant and even-featured, and his smile held a welcome warmth — even a trace of shyness now he and the new nurse were alone together.

Thank heaven for a normal warm-blooded male! breathed Jenni on a sigh of relief. Matt was staring at her with that old familiar look in his admiring black eyes. So I'm not after all totally repugnant. I was beginning to wonder if I'd grown a head of snakes, the way that impossible doctor was carrying on! she thought.

'Drink this, little lady, it surely is nice an' cool straight from the fridge. Ah don't expect you've eaten since break-fast.'

Normally Jenni never touched the stuff, but chilled milk had never been so welcome. She gulped it down like a thirsty child, then paused to ask wonderingly, 'You have refrigerators out here? And showers? Thank heaven! When I got off that bus I thought I'd been dropped in the back of beyond. All I could see was the swirl of dust and a track leading off to goodness knows where. I was trying to summon up the strength to grab my things and start walking when I just flaked out. I don't normally do that,' she added sternly, as if Matt was likely to argue the point.

'No, ma'am,' he agreed civilly, 'but our truck coulda killed you. No one drives fast out here in the bush — never know what's gonna loom up in front of us. All the same, Ross musta got eyes like a hawk to pick you out in all that dust.'

Jenni didn't want to think about Ross McDonnell's eyes. The recollection of their power was like an icy finger tracing the channel of her spine. So he might have killed her! I bet he wished he had, she told herself huffily. Wouldn't that have saved him some aggro?

She drained the plastic beaker and demanded with a frown, 'Dr Blamey, please tell me — is McDonnell some kind of a nut? . . . For some reason I can't fathom, he wants me out of here — he's said so in no uncertain terms.' In his white coat Matt looked far more the professional doctor than Ross McDonnell, and Jenni instinctively felt that here was someone who would take her part.

The hand plucking at Matt's sleeve demanded reassurance. In spite of its pale delicacy it was a workmanlike hand, short-nailed and slightly rough-skinned. 'I'm under contract, for goodness' sake! I asked to come here, specifically. If Ross McDonnell doesn't like the look of me then that's his bad luck. He hasn't the authority to order me back to the UK.' Having got this near to Paul, she promised herself silently, I won't give up, not on some medic's say-so.

The young American pulled a rueful face. The girl kept asking for Father Paul like she couldn't wait another moment to see the guy . . . which was kinda interesting and unexpected. 'You do look — well, like the sun's gonna frizzle you up,' he explained. 'Ross is afraid you ain't gonna cope with the climate. He said he felt sorry for you last night, you looked so washed out. So he left you to sleep in and enjoy the more leisurely bus trip.'

Jenni's jaw dropped. Did Ross really say that?

Some of Matt's pronunciation took a bit of getting used to. Lee-surely . . . not the most obvious description of the ride.

'Oh, Dr Blamey, I'm so tired and confused — ' She gestured helplessly with outstretched hands.

'Uh-uh. Call me Matt. The 'doctor' bit is just a courtesy title. Back home in Alabama Ah'm still in med school,' he told her.

'I thought you looked young to be

qualified,' Jenni hitched herself back up on to the treatment couch and examined Matt Blamey with heightened interest. Here at least was someone she was going to enjoy working alongside. 'Which medical school, Matt?'

'University of New Orleans — yes, ma'am,' he told her proudly, rocking back and forth on his cowboy heels. 'Got another eighteen months before I earn my MD.'

'And you volunteered for this?'

He nodded. 'Yup. Ah'm out here with the American branch of IMR.' Jenni looked blank, and he realised she'd never heard of IMR. 'International Medical Relief. IMR funds people interested in giving some time to medical work in Third World countries. Back in med school Ah'm gonna have to run to catch up, but Ah surely don't begrudge one second. Ah reckon it's the experience of a lifetime, comin' out to help Africa.'

Jenni felt a rush of warmth towards this enthusiastic young man. She thrust forward an eager hand. 'I'm very glad to know you, Matt. Don't let's stand on ceremony — I'm Jenni. Jennifer Westcott.' Her hand was immediately grasped and pumped up and down for several minutes longer than necessary. She made no attempt to withdraw her own hand from Matt's warm clasp, for it was surprisingly comforting to experience friendly physical contact after Dr McDonnell's hostile attitude.

The new nurse had a real cute habit of wrinkling her nose when she smiled, noted the intrigued young American. And good for her, she *could* smile! mused Matt wryly . . . he knew a good few dames who'd have dissolved into tears at being treated with such short shrift by the blunt-spoken Dr McDonnell.

But it was an unfortunate start, that dramatic arrival at the Good Shepherd, coupled with the girl's ultra-feminine appearance. She looked like the kinda chick guys'd make a fuss of and rush to protect.

Small wonder Ross had serious doubts about the wisdom of letting Miss Westcott loose on a remote mission station with three virile white men for company. Matt was including himself, since Charming, his African girlfriend, had gone back to Moshi to complete the midwifery course at the general hospital. Charming's father was a bishop; the Bishop didn't know about Matt. Charming was certain he'd blow his top if he discovered she was in love with a white man.

Sure, Miss Redhead would find more comfort at one of the bigger outfits nearer the coast, but Matt reckoned the new nurse had plans of her own, and these included staying put. She surely would liven the place up!

'C'mon. Ah'll show you where we all hang out.' Matt beat Jenni to the big case and made a face at its weight. If this shrimp could cart a load like this halfway across the world she'd got a navvy's muscles under those pink dungarees!

If Ross is gonna push this chick around, contemplated Matt with a grin, then we're all in for a purty interestin' time. 'This way, ma'am.'

'Yes, Matt,' promised Jenni with happy confidence, gathering up the rest of her stuff, fully recovered now and ready for action, and blithely unaware that concern for her health and strength was not the whole story. 'I intend to work my socks off and show that bully I'm as strong as the other nurses. Two of them are nuns, Sisters from a nursing community, aren't they? Paul said so in his letters . . . '

★   ★   ★

The Mbusa Wa Bwini Mission was Father Paul's 'baby'. Seven years ago, on his arrival as a missionary priest from England, he had been sent here by the diocese of Dar-es-Salaam, under instructions from the African bishop to set up a base in this remote area of bush.

But he had kept regularly in touch with the folks back home in the UK; and especially the Westcott family in whose soot-stained Victorian vicarage he had once lodged. While under their roof he had become engaged to tall serene Helen, the eldest and most tranquil of the three Westcott girls; and it had seemed certain these two would eventually marry when Paul had a parish and a roof of his own to shelter his beautiful blonde fiancée.

To be near Paul, Helen had left her London hospital and taken a staff nurse's post at one of the northern city's general hospitals: and there she had been swept off her sensible feet by a rakish surgeon heading the casualty team!

Within the space of months Helen and Bram Markland were married. And Paul, reacting like the good-natured saint he was, gave the two of them his blessing and not one word of reproach.

Helen's teenage sisters, openly adoring their father's handsome he-man curate, were shocked to the core. Each secretly vowed to grab Paul for herself when his time in Africa was up. But apart from occasional visits on leave, Paul seemed devoted to his new work, and his letters never mentioned the possibility of a permanent return to England.

Hannah's stubborn heart had been captured by a doctor of her own, and in time the only sister whose heartbeat increased at the thought of Paul Hume was Jennifer . . . capricious Jenni, artistic and creative like her mother, whom she resembled physically. But in character Jenni was the cuckoo in the nest. Jenni the dreamer, the wilful one, the stormiest and most temperamental of the three sisters.

Though Jenni had had more boy-friends than Hannah declared *she'd* had hot dinners, Jenni still hadn't found a man to stir her heartbeat like the memory of Paul.

★  ★  ★

The Mbusa Wa Bwini was going from strength to strength.

One of Paul's first actions had been to arrange for weekly visits by a travelling medical team. Young Africans were sent by the theological colleges to learn from the English priest how to run parishes of their own. Mission workers were based there and travelled daily into the bush.

The compound was enlarged to make room next to the tin-roofed Mission church for two buildings for educational use, and an African headmaster was appointed to take responsibility for the school the nuns had started. 'One day,' said Paul with firm conviction, 'we shall withdraw and our African brothers and sisters will take over the Mission. We shall not always be needed here. The time will come for us all to move on.'

The weekly medical visits grew inadequate as word spread and patients overcame their initial shyness, travelling in from a wide radius of village settlements. Paul applied for a small government grant to provide more effective medical cover. Topped up by financial aid from charitable organisations, they were able to set up a proper medical centre with its own dispensary, outpatients and ante-natal clinics; and within the year, when the government made extra funds available, two permanent wards for those too sick to be cared for at home and whose treatment could be carried out on the spot.

To meet the increasing number of mission workers, living accommodation had gradually been extended until the original one-storey wooden bungalow became four sides of a square surrounding an inner courtyard. There was only one entrance, for which Matt and Jenni were now heading across the deserted compound. The air was cooler now, with a smoky tang of wood fires.

Jenni didn't quite know what she had been expecting. But nothing was turning out as in her imaginings. No eager children grasping her skirts — no shy black-skinned mothers dressed in bright *kangas* bringing their babies to greet her. No chatter and colour and noise of welcome for the new white nurse from England. And no Paul. Just the quiet, the stillness, the dull red of the arena of impacted earth and the unpainted wood and stone of the encircling assortment of primitive buildings, only the church easily identifiable in function with its stumpy cross rising from the green-painted corrugated roof and its ever-open door. The pungent smell of wood-smoke hung heavy upon the air.

Where were the villagers Paul had come to work amongst? Where were all their patients? And where, speculated Jenni, a wry frown creasing her freckled forehead, was Ross McDonnell? Her steps dawdled as she examined her new surroundings with curious eyes.

Matt paused for her to catch up, grinning over his shoulder, pointing out the Clinic buildings.

'Goodness! I thought it would be

much bigger than that,' she exclaimed.

'Yeah,' agreed the Southern drawl, 'that was my reaction when I first came. But you can't see the wards from here, or Outpatients or Ante-Natal. They don't face on to the actual compound. It cuts down on traffic to locate entrances round the back. Also encourages patients too timid to come by the main track. The Masai especially prefer it: they're very proud, very secretive people. Come in off the plains but don't never stay long. Won't wait, won't queue.'

'Goodness!' breathed Jenni in excitement. Everyone knew of the Masai, one of the most famous of tribes — formerly very warlike, but now a pastoral people, their whole lives revolving around their cattle.

'Matt?' she queried then.

'Yup?'

'Er — where *is* everyone?'

Matt explained that the African day began early and the children were back in the villages now that it was late afternoon. Jenni gasped — how the day had flown!

Most of the mission workers were out on the field — 'On the field?' 'Just an expression, y'know. You'll hear the trucks coming in soon.'

'It's much cooler now,' said Jenni thankfully. 'I know there's a river somewhere nearby. I've been doing my homework — it must be the big Rufiji. From the bus I could see all the smaller tributaries were bone dry.'

Matt halted at the shallow steps fronting the verandah. He nodded his head in a southerly direction. 'The village is down there above the river bank. That's their cooking fires you can smell. Tomorrow we'll show you round properly — introduce you to the Chief and his wives.'

'Oh, gosh!' said Jenni feebly. 'Me no speaka da lingo. Well, half a dozen words of Swahili which I've mugged up in advance.'

The front door wasn't locked. Jenni didn't suppose anyone bothered with such precautions in a mission; personal possessions would be few in an environment where caring for souls and bodies was all-important. Her own most vital belonging was her hairdryer. The Mission generated its own power supply; she'd checked that out before she came.

She followed Matt along a blank-faced corridor which turned sharp left and presented a row of identical doors facing out on to a long verandah. The central courtyard was open to the sky and strung across with a couple of empty washing lines. 'Here we are. Sister Judith Mary's room, Sister Beatrice, mine — put me among the girls! — and Sylvia's. Ross's pad next door,' said Matt, 'and here's you next to one of the schoolteachers. Brought any whisky with you? Tins of tuna?' he added hopefully. Jenni shook her head. 'Aw, shame.

'The medical staff sleep along this section. It's more convenient and saves disturbing the others when we get called out at night. Paul has his own pad across in the Admin block, but he sometimes uses the room on the corner if we have visitors.

'Your stateroom, ma'am!' Matt bowed and smartly clicked his cowboy heels. Jenni stepped into a small dark cabin of a room. 'Oh-oh! One cockroach bites the dust — ' He swiped at the flimsy interior wall, picked up a corpse between finger and thumb and tossed it past a shuddering Jenni and out through the door.

The room was absolutely basic: a narrow bed made up with clean white sheets and swathed in mosquito netting suspended from an overhead fan. Brown coir matting on the floor, its edges curling dryly in the heat. Beside the bed a Tanzanian three-legged stool with a goatskin seat. Jenni wasn't sure if you were supposed to put your feet on it or what. It was barely a foot high. And to complete the ensemble, one all-purpose cupboard perched on a lopsided table.

'No window!' Jenni reacted with a claustrophobic shiver.

'Sure there is. See, you just unlatch it so-o,' Matt lowered a flap of wood to reveal an oblong of daylight looking out across the verandah to the washing lines in the small courtyard, 'and presto, one window. Usually we close them in the daytime. The flies, y'know. Darn things get everywhere.'

Jenni swallowed bravely. 'But — but there's no glass!'

Matt didn't seem to consider this a deprivation. 'Who needs glass? We all prop our doors open at night anyway. Mosquito netting's more useful than glass in a climate like this.'

'Er — is it all right if I shower?' Jenni was aware that water was always scarce in the inland plateaux, especially in the long dry season when the six months from May to October would see less than an inch of rainfall. 'I feel — er — pretty horrible.'

Matt responded with a gallant, 'Pretty, yup: horrible, no. Sure you can

shower. Middle door across the courtyard. Cold water, though, from a big
tank in the roof. Oh, and don't forget
your robe,' he teased. 'Ross is just along
the way, and man, he misses nothin'!
. . . oh, an' when Big Poppa's truck
pulls in, Ah'll surely tell him you've
arrived safe 'n sound.'

'Big Poppa?' Jenni was scandalised by
the American's irreverence. 'Do you
mean Father Paul?'

Matt grinned cheerfully, displaying
teeth so even they might have been
capped in Beverly Hills: 'Ah surely do.
Ah'm real fond of nicknames, ma'am.
Ross the Boss. Father Paul, Big Poppa
— or just Poppa for short.'

Jenni nodded knowingly. 'And before
very long you're going to come up with
something I'm going to get saddled
with for the rest of my days, right?'

Matt was already on his way. He
swung back to beam at her round the
edge of the door. 'Too right there,
Tadpole,' he agreed, and was gone — to
return seconds later with, 'Supper's at

58

seven. You'll hear the gong. Gotta fly, I'm on duty this evening.'

Great. *Tadpole!* Jenni grimaced in resignation, gazing round her at what looked like the layman's idea of a convent cell, complete with crucifix above a narrow bed adorned with yards of bridal veiling to keep out the mosquitoes. She tested the mattress and winced. Then she recalled that she must shower quickly — and prepare herself for at long *last* seeing Paul again!

Dungarees and T-shirt were deemed too grubby to be dropped on the flimsy brown and cream bedspread. And heaven only knew what other horrible insects lurked in the nooks and crannies or underneath the drab matting which was obviously standard floor covering in the Mission. Jenni rolled the discarded garments into a bundle and shoved them in the cupboard to be dealt with another day.

'*Don't bother to unpack!*' that unpleasant doctor had advised. With an audible sniff she delved into her suitcase and dumped two untidy armfuls on the cupboard shelves. There was no hanging space, but she could manage without. As she rummaged for a couple of towels, her heart began to thud in anticipation. Paul, Paul, Paul — his name rang in her ears. Today seemed more agonising than the whole of the past seven years put together! Would Paul have changed? What would he think of her now? . . . Grown-up. Tamed by the hard work and discipline of the nursing profession. Older and wiser and much more discreet than that teenaged Jenni who wore her youthful adoring heart on her sleeve . . .

Not that Paul had led her on to think —

Oh no, he'd never do that. It was just his nature to be openly demonstrative and affectionate, like the big teasing brother the three sisters had never had. Such a kind and caring man. And handsome as a hero stepped out of the pages of mythology!

The mystery was that he should have

stayed single for so long — evidence, Jenni was certain, of how deeply Helen must have hurt him.

But surely time must have faded Paul's romantic memories of her beautiful sister? And he'd been truly fond of Jenni; if she hadn't been a mere sixth-former he might indeed have consoled himself in her arms.

Oh, but the grown-up Jenni would make it up to Paul for all that unhappiness; he need never be lonely again.

'I thought you'd grown out of all that, you day-dreamer, you,' she teased herself, but with an understanding smile, sliding over bare skin a silky black kimono splashed with peaches 'n cream roses, and belting it tight about her curvy waist. Shuffling size four feet into a pair of elderly espadrilles, she closed her door and ducking under the festoon of washing lines made for the washrooms across the open square.

The showers looked like something out of the Ark. Gingerly Jenni pulled on the chain dangling from a metal lever projecting from the wall. A lethargic gush erupted at shoulder height and caught her slap in the chest, making her gasp involuntarily. She shoved her sticky head directly beneath the spray and shampooed away every trace of heat and dust. Soap ran into her screwed-up eyes, but she was heedless of its sting, sighing with pleasure as the water streamed through her hair and coursed refreshingly over her aching body. It was the first time she'd felt cool and clean since leaving London.

At first she didn't realise that the outer door had been opened and that someone was shouting into the bath-room in a determined bid to attract her attention. When the disagreeable ques-tion penetrated, Jenni switched off the water and peered round the edge of the flimsy shower curtain, pushing the wet hair back from her forehead to discover just who had had the cheek to invade her privacy.

'Are you going to be all night?'

enquired Dr McDonnell in the derisive tones she was coming to know and dislike.

Oh-oh! Jenni's eyes flickered in irritation. Ross the Boss. Or rather head, shoulder, and an impatient hand holding the door sufficiently ajar to allow him to peruse the washroom without actually entering.

'I beg your pardon!' she countered in her haughtiest manner.

'Might have guessed it would be you,' he said, unflatteringly emphasising the 'you'. 'There's half a dozen famished people queueing out here, and *they've* all done a day's work — if you wouldn't mind getting a move on.'

A hand was groping blindly round the folds of transparent nylon shower curtain. There was a pink towel on the bench. 'Is this what you're looking for?'

'I shan't be two minutes. Go away! And shut the door behind you.'

Ross shrugged. 'You could have locked it,' he pointed out with cool logic, but withdrew and left Jenni to finish her ablutions.

If there had been a queue — which she doubted — it had disappeared in the few minutes it took to towel dry. And in spite of his heckling, there was no sign of Ross McDonnell either.

Now Jenni could hear the murmur of voices. Doors stood ajar and windows were flung open to air the stuffy little cabins. And there was the sound of people moving about in their rooms and a woman singing 'The Lord's my shep-he-rd, I'll not want — ' with total unselfconsciousness and a voice that soared like a bird.

Jenni hurried down the passage to the laundry room where Matt had said she would find a power point to plug in her hairdryer. And here she encountered the unlikely source of that rising soprano: a stout-bodied middle-aged woman, short wavy hair streaked with grey, dashing away with the smoothing iron and singing happily as she ironed her starched uniform dresses.

'It is! It must be!' The iron was set

down and Jenni's hands were grasped. 'Jennifer dear!' — both cheeks warmly embraced in spite of her dripping head which shed wet drops over the woman's neat white blouse. 'And here you are, dear, safe and sound, praise the Lord! and come to help us out in our hour of need.'

This was more like it! Just the sort of boost her flagging confidence needed. Jenni brightened visibly.

'We've heard all about you and your darling family,' went on Sister Beatrice, introducing herself with wry humour. 'For my sins I'm the nearest thing we've got to a Matron here.'

She chuckled as Jenni's eyes registered the knee-length navy skirt and cool short-sleeved shirt. 'We don't go in for the traditional nun's habit here in the bush. Do you blame us? Look now, I shan't be offended if you call me Bea. Everyone does.'

Jenni responded thankfully, omitting the embarrassing circumstances of her arrival and saying yes, she'd had a good journey and was raring to start work. Whatever Dr McDonnell might care to imply, she thought with heated indignation, she *was* wanted here at the Mission. He'd surely not be able to get rid of her now. Perhaps the wretched man had been bluffing? But it didn't seem likely. He was so very confident: so very sure of himself. So very much the dominating male.

She plugged her hairdryer into the spare wall socket Sister Bea indicated, her expression thoughtful. It was vital to see Paul before Ross McDonnell could air his prejudices against her.

'What a pretty robe,' the nun was saying. 'Now that's what I miss most about home, the roses!' She could have no idea how the warmth and kindness of her smile was reviving the tired girl finger-drying her damp coppery hair.

Dr McDonnell, declared Jenni's inner voice, you and your ... your *misogynistic* misgivings can just go take a running jump! She switched off and gave her head a shake so that the shining curls tossed in a wild halo.

'Gracious!' exclaimed Sister Bea, who had witnessed the transformation. The steam iron hissed and bubbled as she held it aloft and stared. 'Don't worry,' assured Jenni, misunderstanding, 'I tidy myself up for work.' But tonight, she added silently, I want to look pretty amazing.

★  ★  ★

In her room Jenni decided it would be foolish to risk mascara in the sultry heat of the evening. But she wasn't going to leave well alone. First impressions were what counted . . . and Paul hadn't seen her for almost eight years.

First impressions! Ross hadn't been impressed by *his* first impression of Jenni Westcott, white with dehydration and grubby with dust. Not that she'd been over-impressed with him either — unshaven, sweat-stained, grim-eyed.

Tonight Ross must be shown the London Jenni, the confident, capable woman of the world. Tomorrow he'd see her in action. And though she wasn't anything exceptional, she was a nurse with a heart and a skilled pair of hands. What more did the doctor want?

Jenni Westcott had inherited from her mother not only the delicacy of her colouring but also the sure hand and eye of the artist. Off duty, she chose ice-pink lipgloss, accentuating her hazel-gold eyes with the shimmery pinks and lilacs that few can successfully wear.

Remembering Ross McDonnell's sinister advice about not bothering to unpack more than she would need for one night, Jenni deliberately emptied her cases. She'd hand over the medical supplies tomorrow; to give them to Ross tonight might look like a peace-offering, and her pride would not stoop to that.

She made a rapid decision over dress: not that the choice was extensive. Winter-white legs she concealed in stripy Laura Ashley trousers cut loose

and wide with button-strapped ankles.
And over her head she pulled a cool
jasmine singlet and shoved her uncomfortable bra back into the case.

A hand mirror was all she had to go
on. You'll have to do, *Tadpole*! she
informed her image, firmly closed the
door of her room and ventured out. In
search of her man.

# 3

Jenni had in mind visiting the tin-roofed Mission church. When Paul arrived — and Sister Beatrice said he generally hurried in to say Evensong with the nuns before supper — he would discover her sitting there quietly, waiting for him in the silence.

But on closer inspection the church was not the peaceful oasis she had anticipated. Crossing the compound, Jenni could hear an enthusiastic session of choir practice augmented by African drums, so she changed her plans and veered in the direction of the medical centre where she would be working in less than twelve hours' time. Might be as well to get some idea of the layout.

She was just telling herself that the window on the left, too high to peer through, must belong to that treatment room she'd been dumped in after her wretched 'accident', when a voice rang out behind her from twenty yards away.

'Jenni!'

Jenni froze in her tracks.

It was several seconds before she could bring herself to turn and acknowledge the speaker. Only to realise her mistake, for it wasn't Paul after all but Matt, stethoscope slung round the back of his neck St Elsewhere style, vigorously beckoning her over.

She strolled across, trying to look cool and nonchalant, while a telltale pulse-beat throbbed in her temples.

'Paul's here. He's looking for you. He went thataway.'

'Where's thataway?' Her voice sounded oddly strangulated.

Matt pointed to a battered dust-covered truck parked in the shade of a baobab tree alongside a low mud-brick building. 'You'll find him in his office over there in Admin. Well,' he said in that lazy Southern drawl, 'guess I have a ward round right now. See y'later, Tadpole.'

Admin seemed a grandiose description for the primitive bungalow which was one of the original buildings and served a dual function as office and bed-sits for Paul and his African assistant priest, Father Thomas. Squinting against the last light of day, Jenni's eye followed the direction of Matt's pointing finger and her heart gave a jump of alarm as two tall broad-shouldered men emerged into the sunshine, each dipping his head to avoid the cross-lintel of the door frame. One was the doctor; the other, surpassing even Ross McDonnell for height and breadth, a bearded priest in a white cassock, a lean hand stroking his chin as he listened to what the doctor had to say.

They hadn't noticed her yet. And though she was too far away to hear, Jenni was filled with foreboding. After all, Ross wasn't bluffing. And he'd beaten her to it in bending Paul's ear.

All of a sudden Paul's hearty laughter rang across the compound, a reassuringly familiar sound. What am I worrying about? Jenni chided herself. That's my champion over there! If Paul isn't sticking up for me I'll eat my nurse's cap.

All the same, as she hovered there, mutely observing those two tall powerful-looking figures, she was aware of a sense of acute disappointment. This wasn't how it was supposed to be! The reunion should be private, intimate. Like a seventeen-year-old she had envisaged herself breaking into a run and hurling herself into Paul's outstretched arms. But how could she, with Ross McDonnell not two feet from Paul's side, hands on hips and those hawk eyes swivelling till they rested darkly on the hesitant prey.

Paul's shout broke through her indecision. 'Jenni!' And yes, his arms opened wide, clearly expecting her to come flying across the compound with all the exuberance of the teenager he remembered. His wonderful, kind, encouraging smile never faltered during the long seconds it took for her to reach them, a brave bright answering smile etched on her own face as she willed her legs to take her to him without stumbling.

Ross's expression was indecipherable as he watched the new nurse hurry confidently across and greet Father Paul with uninhibited affection. She looked well enough now; she looked positively fizzing with charm, hugging Paul with eager fervour till it seemed as if her skinny arms would snap, reaching up to kiss him while he stroked her hair and chuckled and hugged her too, as if she were a long-lost relation.

'Well, well, my dearest little Jenni! Let's have a good look at you. Like my very own sister, this one's been to me, you know, Ross.' Paul tweaked a shining copper curl. 'Yes, I just about recognise the hair — but as for the rest of you! My, what a fine figure of a lass, eh, Ross? My dainty Dresden shepherdess has become a pocket Venus!'

A sidelong glance at the doctor, a peep from the safety of Paul's arms.

Triumph flared for one indiscreet moment; just try and get rid of me now! flashed those ecstatic golden eyes.

Jenni lifted her head and returned Paul's laughing scrutiny, and as she drank in the inevitable change in his own appearance her face became solemn and her eyes grew moist. This was . . . this was a much older man than the curly-headed hunk who had teased her in her dreams.

Was Helen to blame? Or was it the strenuous nature of the life Paul had chosen to lead, in an alien climate, so far away from home and those who loved him?

For the past seven years Jenni had carried in her mind's eye the memory of a big blond exuberant Anglo-Saxon hero. Oxford Rugby blue, heart-throb of the parish ladies, macho-idol of Holy Trinity Church youth club. Fittest of the fit, his virile six-feet-and-four clad in tracksuit or cassock or mudcaked rugger shorts. And as kind and compassionate as he was tough.

Darling Paul, agonised Jenni, chewing her bottom lip to ribbons. I never anticipated *you* might have changed. I thought the difference would be in me alone. But you . . . you look thirty-six going on fifty!

Beneath her hands she could feel the broad bones of Paul's shoulders as she raised herself on tiptoe to kiss his hollowed cheek. He might be gaunt, but he still carried the frame of a champion! Some unkind hand had cropped the mop of gilded curls to within an inch of his skull, and seven long hard years had grizzled beard and head with grey. His once golden skin had darkened and weathered, the handsome planes of his face grown disturbingly lean and ascetic. But in spite of the white crinkles formed at their outer edges the eyes hadn't changed: still that familiar heart-piercing blue, still warmed with the love and peace Paul extended to everyone.

Jenni was reminded of pictures of Saint Francis of Assisi. All it needed was for the doves to flutter down out of the gum trees and perch upon his outstretched arms. Paul all clean and ascetic in white. And Dr McDonnell —

From the haven of Paul's arms, Jenni looked back to the other man, and flinched to read the blatant interest in his stare. How could that woman in Dar-es-Salaam have been so mistaken in her description of Ross McDonnell? She'd made *him* out to be some kind of saint, when compared to Paul he was cold, insensitive, and ruthless. Concerned to practise medicine — but with not an ounce of consideration for his colleagues.

Defiantly Jenni tried to stare Ross out, her cheek against Paul's sleeve. So what if he guessed how she felt about the Mission priest?

The doctor, she could hardly fail to notice, had showered and shaved and changed. He certainly looked more . . . civilised. But he was a dangerous man for whom love meant nothing but weakness, derision in his eyes as he observed their affectionate reunion. A man who disliked the look of her and wanted her gone.

She really must talk to Paul in private. 'Can we go inside?' she asked, pointedly ignoring Ross McDonnell and tugging at Paul's leather belt to draw him away.

Ross had seen enough to give him food for thought. His shrewd eyes met Paul's over the girl's head, and his mouth was wry as he heard the Mission priest say, with a wink to the doctor that fortunately Jenni did not see, 'I'll bear in mind what you've told me, Ross. Between us we can work something out.'

Once they were alone Jenni did a dreadful and most uncharacteristic thing. She burst into tears. It was the change in Paul, the evidence of the wrong her sister had done him.

She's overwrought, he thought compassionately; it's been a long day — my poor little Jenni!

In his office Paul sat Jenni on a chair

78

and hitched up one side of his cassock to reveal startlingly brown legs in a pair of brief beige shorts, whose pockets he was exploring for a handkerchief. Jenni's emotions seemed to have got quite out of control. Giggles spluttered through her tears, but she did as she was told and gave her nose a good hard blow.

'I'm going to take this off, since it's making you laugh. The Sisters can manage Evensong without me tonight — it's not every day Jennifer Westcott comes out to Africa.'

Jenni's voice was muffled in the hankie. 'Sorry about this, Paul. I think I must have got a touch of the sun — but please, please, take no notice of whatever Ross McDonnell's been making out. I'm tough as old boots and I refuse — to go — back.' The words trailed away as she gazed at the still-powerful build now accentuated by clinging white T-shirt and cuffed khaki shorts. Paul's feet were bare and he had obviously recently changed into open leather sandals, because thick socks and dusty boots lay discarded on the floor just inside the door.

Yes, he had changed physically. But once over the initial shock she wasn't sure that he hadn't become even more devastating as a result. If Helen could see Paul now!

Mustn't think such things! Jenni scolded herself, scandalised by the way her imagination sometimes ran riot. My sister's got three children! When Paul and I are married I shall devote my life to making it up to him. We'll have lots of babies and they'll all be the image of their father . . .

'Penny for your thoughts, young woman!' teased Paul, his expression fondly reminiscent as the golden-hazel eyes drifted off into a world of their own. Young Jenni hadn't changed so much after all, ever the dreamer, still the romantic. And, true enough, she did look perfectly healthy and well able to cope with nursing at the Mission. She'd always been pale as milk and on the small side, but nurses weren't required to be of Amazon proportions.

She'd certainly filled out in all the right places too. Paul smiled and scratched his beard. Wouldn't Matt be goggling when he clapped eyes on her in that outfit? Should help to take his mind off Charming's transfer to Moshi.

'I'll be entirely responsible for her, Ross,' he had promised confidently. 'She won't be a liability, not our Jen, and her appearance is very deceptive. Never was a one for the soft option either — she had the talent to get into art school but insisted on nursing. Anyway, if she's made up her mind to do something, heaven help the man who tries to stop her! Spirited trio, those Westcott girls . . . wonderful family — I can't tell you how kind those parents were to me.'

Paul was more used to having others confide in him. But there was something about Ross McDonnell — some quality of strength of character that in spite of the short time the doctor had been working at the Mission had convinced Paul here was a man you could trust with your life.

'I've never mentioned this before, but I — '

He couldn't do it. He bit back the words. To reveal that broken engagement seemed churlish now that Helen was the mother of another man's children.

And Ross, who had not missed the hesitation, wondered what secrets of the past this girl would stir up with her presence.

* * *

Supper was bewildering. Endless introductions, names to match to faces, peculiar food . . . Jenni's face ached with smiling. And to cap it all, when she made her excuses and crept off early while everyone else was lounging about, playing chess and Scrabble and drinking endless cups of coffee as they dissected another day's work (obviously a post-prandial ritual among the Mission staff), who should step out of the shadows to escort her across the ill-lit compound but Ross McDonnell.

'I think you and I should have a little talk.'

About to complain that she was bone-weary, Jenni bit the words back, straightened her shoulders and tried to look alert and ready for anything. At the same time her spirits were at rock bottom. Not a moment of physical weakness would she dare permit herself when working with Dr McDonnell. He was just the sort to round on her with an 'I told you you weren't up to the job' gleam in his nasty eye.

'If it's about your kind offer to drive me back to the coast in the morning,' she retorted, insolent with fatigue, 'forget it. I'm not going. And you can't make me!'

It was a foolish sort of challenge to issue to any man. But to one who had formed such a low opinion of her it was worse than foolish. Ross was reining in his temper on a very short leash: even in the dark the atmosphere between them crackled with hostility.

'Don't come whining to me when you develop sunstroke,' he gritted. 'I've arranged with Paul to give you a fortnight's trial. But as far as I'm concerned you're here on sufferance.'

Jenni choked with rage. She could feel her scalp tingle with redheaded passion. 'A fortnight's *trial*? I trust you're joking, Dr McDonnell!' Her thoughts rattled furiously. How *dared* he sit in judgment on an experienced RGN! The College of Nursing, so generously helping fund her stay, would have a fit if she reported this back. 'I've got a post-registration paediatric quali-fication and I've taken a special course in nutrition at the London School of Tropical Medicine.' They had reached the out-of-the-way corner that housed the generator and she raised her voice shrilly above its ceaseless engine noise. 'I have my own work to do out here. So if you were thinking I'd be your dogsbody then you're in for a disappointment!'

'Keep your hair on,' sneered Ross, complimenting himself on controlling an overwhelming desire to drag this troublesome young woman into one of those tempting black spaces between the shadowy buildings and throttle her good and proper. 'The College,' he continued patronisingly, his deep voice so redolent of power and male authority, 'wouldn't fund you if you were useless. But as the saying goes, if you can't stand the heat then it's prudent to keep out of the kitchen. Rest assured it's your physical well-being we have in mind, rather than the level of your competence!'

Grrrr! Silently Jenni ground her teeth. That 'we' was a masterly touch. And he knew more than she'd given him credit for. A dangerous man to tangle with, Ross McDonnell.

She swayed slightly, suddenly aware of feeling limp as a rag. This unwelcome confrontation had drained the last of her resources.

The doctor's forearm brushed hers just above the elbow, and she flinched as the fleeting contact gave rise to a burning sensation searing through her skin to the underlying nerves. She moved a pace to the left and wondered whether he intended to escort her to the door of her room. What was he afraid she'd get up to, then, left to her own devices? Creep off to Admin and secrete herself in Paul's bed?

Perhaps he was jealous! A virile doctor with middle-aged nuns for company. No wonder he was so ratty, considered Jenni with a woozy smirk, almost tripping over her own feet again.

They came to the verandah steps. Ross bade her a terse good night.

'Report to Sister Beatrice first thing in the morning. And try to keep in the shade as much as possible until you get acclimatised. You know where you are now — ' Like a gaoler he was waiting to see her enter the doorway, a foot lodged on the bottom step, his shadow menacingly huge against the fitful flickering light.

'Let's hope a night's sleep will put you in a civil mood tomorrow. I look forward to that.'

He turned abruptly and strode off into the shadows, apparently heading out of the compound and in the direction of the distant river.

Deprived of the last word, Jenni went seething to her room, where, switching on the ceiling fan to stir the sultry air, she emptied her case and hung up her white cotton uniform ready for duty on the morrow.

The day dawned cool and pleasant and saturated with the smell of strange shrubs, the air full of jubilant birdsong. A shy black girl in a red dress several sizes too big brought bowls of hot water to each room. Jenni had slept like a top and been awakened by a nearby radio tuned to the BBC World Service. 'Dammit, I keep getting Radio Moscow!' complained a disembodied voice through the cardboard-thin walls.

Someone on the other side was viciously slapping at cockroaches.

The morning clouds glowed red and gold, and Jenni felt absurdly happy and excited as she hurried across to breakfast. Some were tucking into fried food, but all she required was a steaming cup of coffee to dispel the shivers and some delicious fresh paw-paw, with a squeeze of lime, to get the juices flowing. 'Good luck!' encouraged Paul in passing, squeezing her shoulder warmly. 'Tell me all about it this evening.'

Though she looked for them, there was no sign of Ross or Matt Blamey.

Thinking rather longingly of those red-lined woollen capes nurses back home take for granted, Jenni headed for the building glamorised with the name of 'hospital'. The Red Cross truck was gone and the parking space beneath the baobab tree was empty. Peculiar trees, mused Jenni, squinting at the huge swollen water-storing trunk and flat-tened crown.

Most of the European staff, medical and missionary, had been introduced during supper — except for Sylvia Anstey who was taking a turn on night duty, with a newly enrolled African nurse to help her. Ross seemed to be on permanent call. Grudgingly Jenni had to concede that the doctor was certainly setting himself a tough pace for the duration of his East African contract.

She found Sylvia and Bea in the small office that linked the two wards. Bea was welcoming, Sylvia less so. Jenni noticed that she didn't bother with a cap or tights and that on her feet she was wearing a pair of Scholls sandals. She was a tall girl, in her late twenties, with sun-streaked brown hair that had been short when she arrived at the Mission two years back, but which she'd given up trying to cut herself and was attempting to scrape back into an unsuccessful ponytail. Her features were handsome rather than pretty and her skin, noted Jenni with a pang of envy, had an even golden quality that wouldn't freckle in a month of sunny Sundays.

Sylvia looked nice: but she didn't seem very friendly. Perhaps, wondered Jenni sadly, Ross had already put in a bad word for her with his staff. No one would relish working with the new nurse at this rate.

Sylvia disappeared with alacrity when Bea, having heard the night report, suggested she hop off and grab some breakfast before her snoozetime. 'I'll take Jennifer round with me now. Oh, before you go, Sylvia, how did you find Nurse Ndogo? She only came to us last month, Jennifer, and this was her first time here on nights.'

'Apparently she's done a lot of night duty during her training at the General Hospital in Moshi. A bit slow, perhaps — but then all the Africans take their time over things. I had to bully her a bit to keep her awake, but she's willing enough and competent in all the basic procedures. I'd be fairly happy to leave her in charge after a few weeks.'

'Aha,' said Bea, 'that's what we want to hear. The ultimate aim,' she explained to the alert-eyed Jenni, 'will be to withdraw and let the Africans take responsibility for their church and hospital. Paul drums this into everyone continually. We mustn't kid ourselves we're indispensable.'

Jenni was telling herself that the nun looked exactly like a nurse from the forties in her white dress and short veil, fob watch pinned to an expanse of plump frontage and her stoutish legs in thick support stockings. 'The heat plays murder with my varicosities,' said Bea in tones of cheerful uncomplaint, waggling a Clarks-sandalled foot. Conscious of the sickly pallor of her own legs, Jenni too was wearing stockings. Given half a chance she'd try for a tan. It would be OK if she lay under a bush with her legs sticking out and thickly smeared in high-factor sun cream.

'Wherever have you put all that hair, dear?' queried Bea, peering around Jenni's neat white disposable cap.

Jenni laughed. 'Years of practice, Sister Bea. It looks a complicated sort of plait, but I can manage it even in the dark in about twenty seconds.'

'Do I hear someone crying? — come along and I'll show you our children's ward.'

The nurses walked into a hub of chatter with perhaps nine or ten children laughing and splashing as they were given their morning baths in big tin tubs. Two girls in yellow overalls covered by plastic pinafores were supervising the proceedings, helped by the women who squatted on mats among the cots: mothers, sisters, aunts — whoever could be spared to stay with a sick and frightened child.

Morning sunshine streamed in through the windows, and though the room was overcrowded and not much bigger than a large bedroom, it was cheerful and fresh with white walls and blue paintwork. A sugar-paper frieze, drawn by the Sunday School and gaily depicting African village life, ran all round the walls to brighten the stay of children who had to be kept overnight, or longer, for treatment. Wherever possible, explained Bea, they were allowed home. If seriously ill and beyond the help of the Mission doctors, they would be transferred by ambulance to the General Hospital in Moshi.

A tiny boy with matchstick-thin limbs, a swollen stomach and soap in his eyes, was sobbing piteously. Heedless of her uniform, Jenni scooped him out of the bath and comforted him with soothing noises.

The scene was a news still become three-dimensional . . . a lump rose in Jenni's throat. Her thoughts grew muddled by emotion. If she had believed she had come only to see Paul again, then she had been deceiving herself. Here at last were the children she had yearned to work amongst. And paediatric nursing was the special skill she could offer.

Suddenly, his eyes free of soap, the

child examined Jenni in alarm and held his arms out to Sister Bea, keening to be rescued from this strange being. The other children grew quiet and they too latched on to Jenni with timid, lustrous eyes. The mothers stopped their chattering and stared. One of the helpers took the boy and after delivering a smacking kiss to each tear-stained cheek wrapped him in a dry towel, saying, 'Come on, silly baby!'

'Bea? — whatever is it?' Jenni's face was anxious and her freckles stood out against the pallor of her skin.

'Don't fret — they think your head's on fire. Touch your hair and keep smiling. Show them it isn't hot!'

Bea spoke rapidly in a tribal dialect, her words incomprehensible to Jenni, but the tone of her voice like any mother's coaxing a smile from a troubled child. The children giggled and shy smiles broke out. Reaching into a recovery cot, Bea handed Jenni a baby with bandaged eyes who dabbed sightlessly at her freckles and discovered instead her tiptilted nose, crowing with delight.

'Ross operated on this little chap before he left for Dar. And those two over there. Congenital cataracts — tragically commonplace in this part of the world.'

The baby clung to her and with regret Jenni lowered him back into his cot, planning to come back and cuddle the child the first opportunity she got. Where was his mother? He seemed quite alone. She went round to each child, helping with a T-shirt here, straightening a cotton blanket there, holding a small head while a thirsty mouth slurped water from an enamel mug, stroking a sticky brow and all the while smiling, '*Jambo!* Hello. *Jambo!*' to the women crouching nearby.

Bea was busy instructing the local girls she was training in basic nursing care. When she had finished she beckoned Jenni to her side.

'Through here you'll find the kitchen

and the sluice, and beyond them the Out-patients' Room and our mini-marvel OR and the autoclave room.' Sister indicated for Jenni to go ahead. She was still eulogising on the theme of Ross McD.

'I cannot tell you what a blessing it is having an eye surgeon of such calibre here. It'll break my heart to let dear Ross go back to Liverpool! — but there, we should be grateful he cared enough to come to us in the first place. And I get the impression,' said Sister confidingly, 'he needed to get away for a while. Personal circumstances. Not that Ross is a man to air his washing in public, though he'd find nothing but understanding at the Mission. Goodness only knows but we've all got skeletons in our cupboards.'

Talking of cupboards reminded Jenni that she'd left the vaccines and stuff in hers. She must hand them over today, for hadn't the parish striven like the dickens to raise funds to send out extra medical supplies?

'I sense he may have known deep unhappiness,' sighed Bea, opening the door of the cubbyhole that served as a sluice. 'Sometimes I see a look in his eyes that makes me wonder if . . . Not quite like you're used to, dear, but it serves, it serves. The kit for the urine tests you'll find in the cupboard above the sink.'

Jenni concealed an ironic twitch of the lips with a tactful hand. Privately she suspected the good Sister of reading too many romances and neglecting her Bible. Anyway, Jenni didn't feel able to dredge up much sympathy for Dr McD. If anyone had suffered, it was Paul; but no one here seemed to know anything about the broken engagement, and she, Jenni, was not about to gossip of having a sister who had done something no woman could be proud of.

All the same, it was interesting to speculate. Had some professional crisis driven Ross McDonnell to pack scalpel and ophthalmoscope and head for Africa? Or was it a private affair, involving a woman?

Paul might know. He was a man others felt driven to confide in.

'Our layout here would make an architect's hair stand on end,' said Bea with cheerful unconcern. 'If we've got enough money we just tack on another section. Anyone and everyone mucks in to help. We even learned to make our own bricks from the red soil. Father Paul's worked like a Trojan himself, putting up new buildings with his bare hands.' She bustled ahead. 'Now these are the two adult wards. Sister Judith Mary is in charge here. And there's Dr Blamey taking samples for tests . . . I don't think we'll disturb them, dear, do you? You can pop in later. Have a quick peep in the Out-patients' Room. Dr Ross has a clinic in here tomorrow afternoon. Sylvia usually works with him, but of course she's on nights this week, so I'll be asking you to take that job over.'

'Of course, Sister,' responded Jenni, who had been brought up never to shirk an assignment, however distasteful.

'Now, while I supervise breakfasts, you have a nose round on your own and see where our equipment is stored. Then when you've got your bearings you'll be ready to get cracking. I'm afraid you're going to have to accept a flexible schedule.'

'That's fine with me, Sister,' agreed Jenni cheerfully.

Beatrice patted her arm, 'Good girl,' she said approvingly, and hastened on her crêpe-soled way.

DISPENSARY, read the black lettering on the opposite door. Thinking it was surely too early for anyone to be in there working, Jenni tested the handle, expecting to find the place securely locked. Nothing of the sort.

She found herself peering inquisitively into a small but efficient laboratory. Three walls were fitted with waist-high lockable cupboards, ranks of bottles lining the open shelves above, neatly stacked cartons and dispensing paraphernalia conveniently to hand.

A work bench ran the length of the window wall, with an inset sink at which a tall young African in a lab coat was washing his hands. 'Er — Mr Mwinyi!' He nudged the head dispenser who was seated on a high stool examining slides under a microscope.

'CDM?' wondered Jenni aloud, reading out the mysterious initials on a huge bottle of liquid mixture.

'Children's Diarrhoea Mixture.' Mr Mwinyi peered over gold-rimmed bifocals at the intruder. 'Nurse Westcott!' His face lit up in a broad grin of recognition. He had greying hair and an enormous mouth of widely spaced teeth. 'Come right on in, if you please, Nurse. Permit me to introduce my most able assistant, Kefa.'

The young man was clearly shy of Jenni and retreated from the warmth of her handshake into work. Reaching self-importantly for a tablet counter, he began refilling small plastic containers, all the while darting sidelong glances at this vision in nurse's uniform. Jenni looked apologetic and insisted she hadn't meant to interrupt.

First wiping his hands on his white coat, the dispenser wrung her hand and reminded her that they had met at supper the previous evening. 'How nice to see you again, Mr Mwinyi,' said Jenni hastily, afraid she might have given offence. 'You must forgive me for not immediately recognising you. In the past twenty-four hours I've been introduced to about fifty different people!'

'And we Africans all look alike,' suggested Francis Mwinyi with a humorous twinkle in his eye. 'Now, miss, please sit here and view for yourself this slide. You are of course regularly taking the malaria pills? Good. I shall show you a typical example of *plasmodium vivax*, colloquially known as the malarial parasite.'

Obediently Jenni hoisted herself up on to his stool and adjusted the microscope's eyepiece to suit her slightly short-sighted vision. She had examined such slides as part of her nutrition course, which included an introduction to tropical diseases, but did not wish to give offence by saying so.

The morning sped by with scarcely a moment to think of Paul. Ross McDonnell, she discovered, had set off at daybreak for his weekly visit to a distant riverside village where he was treating all the children for bilharzia, contracted from playing in the murky larvae-infested waters. In her lunch break Jenni sat on the verandah with her feet stuck out into the sunshine and her legs shiny with cream, a sketchpad on her lap as she made swift charcoal drawings of the schoolchildren playing in the compound.

The teacher on playground duty wagged a reproving finger when a straying football thudded against the dispensary window. Jenni smiled to herself and deftly included the teacher in her scene. A group of little girls in bobbing cotton skirts — she judged them to be about seven or eight years old — whirled red and yellow hoops round and round their waists and skinny legs, counting loudly in English — 'five, *six*, seven, *eight*'. While a crocodile of tiny tots, playing Follow my Leader and skipping in and out among the buildings, got tangled up in the older boys' cricket — a game taken very seriously indeed, judging by the protesting cries of the enthusiastic team as the squealing children trundled heedlessly past the stumps someone had painted for them on the school wall.

Paul's handiwork, guessed the amused artist. He'd always been crackers about all kinds of sport. No need for a PE master in this school.

Fascinated with seeing the children at play, Jenni watched, her sketchpad slipping forgotten from her lap. When the headmaster, a tall young African wearing serious-looking spectacles, came out of the school with a handbell, the chatter and laughter ceased on the instant as

103

the children formed orderly lines and marched back to their classrooms. Jenni glanced at her watch. Ten more minutes' break: then the nurses were going to get ready for the ante-natal clinic.

The compound settled into a sultry stillness, the doves dozing in the gum trees, just the buzz of a distant motor — probably the bus, running an hour or so earlier today. She stretched and yawned, wriggled her warm toes and viewed her legs with a critical eye. *Still*, botheration, a whiter shade of pale . . .

Next instant the peace was shattered by a dreadful commotion, a man screaming horribly with pain. And it seemed to come from behind the kitchens. 'One of the cooks,' gasped Jenni, 'must have scalded himself!' Struggling to push hot sticky feet back into shrunken shoes, she glanced wildly round for help. A nurse! A doctor! Someone, please . . . Oh, lor', *I'm* a nurse —

She took the verandah steps in one leap, almost tumbling flat on her face, regained her balance and set off at a gallop. Faces appeared at doors and windows, amazed to see the nurse they had already christened 'the fire woman', capless, her amazing hair tumbling over her shoulders; dashing through the red dust towards Bwana Mac, who was half carrying, half dragging a writhing African whose groans of *Uchavi! Uchavi!* echoed round the compound.

Between the two of them, doctor and nurse got the poor fellow into the treatment room where twenty-four hours ago Jenni herself had received scant sympathy at the hands of Ross McDonnell.

'Stay with him,' barked Ross, striding off to the dispensary where he went into rapid consultation with Francis Mwinyi.

The African had meanwhile refused the treatment couch and squatted in a corner on the goatskin seat of a native stool barely a foot off the ground, bony legs in flapping cotton trousers bent double and his shirt concertinaed about his middle.

'*Uchavi!*' he continued to moan, and Jenni, feeling worse than useless, could do no more than wipe away the pearls of sweat running down into his eyebrows. What on earth had possessed her to think she could swan out here and do her Florence Nightingale act with people she could not even *begin* to communicate with?

All the same, she was driven to try, crouching down and putting her arm across the poor fellow's thin, shuddering shoulders, trying to make the tone of her voice as calm and reassuring as possible. 'The doctor — Mganga — he will make you better.'

Ross's legs suddenly appeared in her line of vision. They were coated with dust again. It didn't take five minutes to get in that state, she now realised, and in shorts he certainly had an impressive pair of hard-muscled thighs.

'What's the matter with him? What is this — *uchavi*?' she queried.

'He thinks he's been poisoned — some quarrel in his village with another man. I found him by the roadside, trying to drag himself here.'

'Poison?' Jenni repeated, consternation all over her expressive freckled face. 'Oh, good grief!' A British doctor couldn't possibly know the antidote for a witch doctor's lethal concoction.

Assuming water was all Ross had to offer, Jenni reached up to take the enamel mug from him. But to her hurt surprise he brushed her aside so roughly that a few drops splashed down the front of her uniform. Starting at the sensation of cool liquid on bare skin, she glanced down at herself in some surprise — and with mortification realised why the doctor had rebuffed her helping hand.

Clearly he supposed this unseemly display of cleavage was for *his* benefit — and wished to demonstrate that he was not impressed, either by her vital statistics or her timing! And who could blame him?

'Sorry,' muttered Jenni, fastening the poppers down her front. 'I was sunbathing, but when I heard this poor man . . . I just ran.'

Ross didn't need to comment. A glance upward from under golden eyelashes showed Jenni his thoughts writ clear all over his sardonic face . . . *Sun*bathing! Daft little freckled Pom, you won't last five minutes out here!

'*Dawa ya nguvu!* — powerful medicine!' Ross squatted down beside the patient.

Groaning inwardly because of her careless tongue, Jenni watched as their patient swallowed the drink as if it were his last, with great gurgling gulps, his hands shaking so much that Ross had to hold the mug to his lips. When every drop was drained, the sick African fell back against the wall, exhausted.

'What happens now?' Jenni didn't relish witnessing the dying spasms of a poisoned man.

With surprising gentleness Ross lifted

the thin figure bodily and placed him, unresisting now, on the treatment couch. Ross said nothing, made no attempt to give a civil answer to her question, but for the next three minutes watched intently as the body relaxed, the head sank on to the pillow and the man's groans changed to sighs of relief.

At last the doctor spoke, and his voice was quiet with a relief of his own that Jenni readily shared. 'He'll be OK. We can leave him to sleep it off and then he can go back to his home.'

He opened the door and waited for Jenni. 'Time to get the next show on the road, eh, milkmaid? — all those mums-to-be queueing up to see us. Better go and fetch your sunshade.'

I shall not rise to your cheap jibes, sniffed Jenni, her resolute nose in the air. You want me to lose my temper and give you the satisfaction of a blazing row, then you'll turn round and tell Paul I don't fit in with this precious team. Well, Ross the Boss, you're going to be disappointed.

Because I'm determined to defy my own nature and stay cool — until I've been here long enough to prove my worth. After that, sir, you can expect the fur to fly. Because I've a temper as fiery as my hair: and if I have to suppress my frustration over-long then when the time comes I shall ex-*plode*!

# 4

'If it's not a rude question,' said Jenni at supper that night, 'may I ask what I'm eating?'

Paul told her it was goat's meat stew. 'We get quite a lot of this,' he said, lowering his voice to add with a wink, 'unfortunately! I'm a shadow of my former self. Twelve and a quarter stone. Seconds, Ross? — the pace you set, you need all the calories you can get.'

The doctor raised an eyebrow but shook his head.

Jenni smiled sympathetically at Ross, sitting opposite her at the long trestle table. 'Like eating stringy chewing gum, isn't it!'

Matt, who would have tucked heartily into rhino and chips if it had been on the menu, looked up from his laden plate and guffawed. 'You're dead right there, baby!'

111

They were serving themselves from a huge stewing pot, adding a helping of the thick maize porridge called *ugali*. Matt passed along a dish of sliced carrots and spinach. 'Try some of this — it's real good.'

Paul looked wistful. 'When I first came out here, what I missed most was Jenni's mother's home cooking. Ah, those homemade soups and Irish stews simmering on the Rayburn!'

It was what she had been specially looking forward to, recalling the old days. But whenever Paul spoke of her family she sensed the doctor's acute, silent interest — and it both puzzled and disturbed her. Again she was aware of those astute deep-set eyes, settling their heavy gaze upon her, crushing her slim appetite and making her wary of every word — every thought, even! — for no accountable reason.

Well, no, that was hardly the case: she knew the reason well enough. Ross McDonnell was speculating about matters which were no concern of his, trying to see inside her head and suss out what was going on between her and dear *wonderful* Paul. The cheek of it! It wasn't as if Paul was a monk who had taken special vows or anything.

'All credit to the Sisters,' Paul was informing the table at large, 'who've done a very creditable job in training our cooks and improving the menus. Last night's supper was a treat. The occasional lapse is good for the soul.'

Sister Judith Mary clasped her hands and exclaimed, 'Sole! — that's what I could eat right now: grilled Dover sole with a crisp green salad.'

Such irreverence from the angular, bespectacled Sister Judith Mary reduced Jenni to a fit of the giggles. Ross McDonnell's scrutiny was making her nervous, and it was a peculiar and unfamiliar feeling, like being an inexperienced teenager again. What was he doing? Counting the freckles he so disapproved of?

Declining the fresh dates, she slipped away from the table and to calm herself down went over to the small library of paperbacks shelved in a quiet corner of the L-shaped room.

Here was the one place in the Mission which conjured up visions of old Colonial days. A touch of the Somerset Maughams, with ceiling fans and spindly bamboo tables, earthenware pots of huge Kentia palms and basket chairs lined with faded batik cushions.

Jenni picked out a dog-eared E. M. Forster novel and settled in one of the creaky chairs.

'What's that you're reading?'

Ross's hand closed firmly over her own and tilted the book's cover towards the light. He snorted with laughter.

Jenni was puzzled. She peered again at the title and winced. *Where Angels Fear To Tread.* How unfortunate!

She heard the creak of wickerwork as the doctor settled himself beside her. 'I brought your coffee over,' he said amiably.

Her acknowledgement was polite but terse. Everyone else was out of earshot.

What did he want with her? Why couldn't he leave her in peace?

'That was a rum do, that *uchavi* business,' observed Ross conversationally.

Jenni didn't respond, recollecting the abrupt way she'd been pushed aside when they were dealing with the poisoned African. Another memory brought a faint blush of rose to her pale cheeks. Instinctively her fingers touched the pearl buttons of her white silk shirt, checking that all was secure on the Westcott front. How preposterous of Ross McDonnell to think she was being deliberately provocative, running around half-dressed. No doubt he was used to more adoring nurses back home.

She was going through the motions of page-turning, acutely conscious of Ross's proximity. He was flicking through a Graham Greene, the sprawl of his long legs almost brushing her white skirts.

No indeed, considered Jenni, taking a

surreptitious glance at his strong profile, you're not as handsome and saint-like as darling Paul. Yet you are a powerfully attractive man and you have a very unsettling effect on me.

Her thoughts wandered on. You work punishingly hard, Dr Mac. Dealing with all those pregnant women in the ante-natal clinics. Immunising thousands of children against measles. All the African problems — malaria, cholera, tuberculosis, polio, to name but a few. Doesn't it ever get you down, doctor? So many serious conditions we rarely come across back home. And as if that were not enough, your eye surgery programme as well. As hard and as fast as you work, doctor, you can't help more than a tiny percentage. So doesn't it depress you?

You waste no time: and you waste few words! Though as Bea pointed out when *I* commented that Hello, How are you? and Goodbye wasn't *wildly* friendly, you don't have the command of Swahili that would make communication easier. OK, Dr Mac, considering you have to be a Jack-of-all-trades out here, you do a pretty fair job. But secretary of your fan club I shall never be.

'Thought so — I've read it.' Ross dropped the paperback on the table and turned sideways in his chair, leaning an elbow on the wicker arm and rubbing his chin with his thumb. With parted lips Jenni pretended a deep interest in page seventeen, but that didn't deter him from interrupting. 'How did you find it this afternoon, all that heat?'

'More to the point,' she countered spiritedly, 'how did you find it? At least I was under cover with the notes and record cards. You seemed to be out there squatting among the women for ages with the sun beating down on you.'

Ross was typically dismissive. 'No problem. But you're looking a trifle pink to me. Specially those legs.'

Jenni pulled the folds of her full skirt over her glowing calves and deliberately focused her gaze on Paul, holding forth in the midst of a chattering group of Mission workers. Ross followed the direction of her eye and remarked pointedly, 'So Hume's known you since you were sweet sixteen.' Too young then, he observed to himself, but not too young now . . .

For the first time it occurred to Jenni how unwise she had been in her blatant display of affection for Paul. To the doctor it must seem obvious now that the new nurse had come out there in pursuit of the Mission priest, for all the wrong reasons as far as the single-minded Ross McDonnell was concerned. No wonder his eyes were so wary, so glinting with disapproval!

Jenni swallowed in agitation and wondered how on earth she was going to convince Ross of the integrity of her motives. Yes, she wanted Paul to marry her; but for some strange reason that over-whelming purpose had already receded to second place. The medical set-up was fascinating. Work was foremost now in her mind.

There was no urgency any more where Paul was concerned. It's as if, mused Jenni, we both know it's inevitable, it's going to happen, we can take our time, get to know each other again at our own pace. Oh, how I'd love to tell Ross about the broken engagement to Helen, just to see the look on his face. He wouldn't be so sure of himself then.

'That was an odd business,' repeated Ross, 'that poor chap who thought he'd been poisoned.'

Jenni's ears pricked up. 'Thought? You mean — But you administered the antidote?' Her puzzled eyes swung from Paul and back to Ross, who shrugged and gave a rueful lopsided grin.

He looked younger when he smiled, less dour, and the steely quality of his gaze was momentarily softened. 'I'd no idea what was wrong with him,' Ross admitted candidly. 'We have to thank Francis Mwinyi for getting us out of what could have been a very nasty situation. As it was, I had a tense moment or two waiting to see what the outcome was going to be . . .

'Sorry, by the way, to spill that stuff down your uniform. It shouldn't be a permanent stain. I couldn't risk letting you give the drug and taking the brunt if the man should die. We might well have had the *mchawi* stirring up the relatives by claiming we were the ones who'd poisoned him. And it was far better if any trouble was directed at me.'

For once Jenni was at a loss for words. Shamefacedly she fussed with the heavy waves spilling over her temples. You idiot! She squirmed in self-ridicule. Ross never even noticed your buttons were undone . . . he was too busy protecting you from possible repercussions. Jumping to hasty conclusions yet again, Hothead Westcott — Let this be a lesson to you.

'And had he been poisoned?' she managed eventually.

Ross gave a shrug of broad khaki

shoulders. He scratched the sunburned column of his throat and said that in his view it could well have been a case of extreme hysteria; but to be on the safe side the mug of water had been laced with tincture of opium.

'Did I hear someone mention poison?'

Paul had wandered across to pick up the tail end of this conversation. He drew up a chair while Ross explained what had occurred.

A chilly shudder ran through Jenni's frame. 'I didn't realise witch doctors still existed!'

'Ah, indeed they do. But you must differentiate between the *mganga* or local medicine man — who, it must be admitted, still exercises a very powerful influence within the tribes — and the *mchawi,* or wizards, who practise black magic and are decidedly more dangerous.'

Lamplight accentuated the harsh lines etched into the planes and hollows of the priest's grave countenance. He gestured with long-fingered hands as he spoke. 'We as Christian missionaries are working amongst a fearful and superstitious people who believe that during *usiku* — the hours of darkness — dangerous spirits roam the land and magic is rife. There's a world of anxiety here in the bush. You've noticed it yourself, haven't you, Ross? How they mull over your every word and expression: 'Did the doctor frown when he was speaking to me? Is that why I'm not getting better?' They love and fear you at one and the same time.'

Ross was nodding, and his face mirrored Paul's grimness. Jenni sat very still.

She was beginning now to have some inkling of the complex nature of Paul's work in Africa. It wasn't how she'd imagined it — a simple matter of going round preaching and everyone seeing the light and saying 'Praise the Lord!' Here was a challenge far more profound than some love affair that had gone wrong. No wonder Paul was physically altered, no wonder he had grown contemplative and . . . and . . .

Wise, decided Jenni in awe. It was no longer so easy to picture him as a married man with a wife and family of his own. The children of the bush were his children; their families were his families. She had a peculiar feeling that he would never want to leave Africa and come home — and that suspicion gave rise to a disquiet she hastily pushed to the back of her mind, to be worried over in total privacy, some other time.

'Well, our Jen, are you glad you came?'

'Oh yes!' she said fervently.

This was followed by an awkward silence. Ross was bound to consider her gushing and ingenuous if she babbled on about why she was so sure, so soon, that she'd made the right decision in coming to Africa. Sure about the satisfactions of her work; far less certain, though, about her relationship with Paul.

Ross was flicking through the pages of Punch, but Jenni knew he'd be listening and ready to pounce. 'I'm not being a great deal of use at the moment,' she acknowledged — well, if she didn't say it first, to be sure Ross would! During the afternoon session, whenever the doctor had asked for a specific item — a pair of surgical gloves to replace the ones he'd just split, a tongue depressor — while she had bumbled around uncertainly, one of the African helpers had brought what Papa Mganga required within seconds.

Ross quirked an eyebrow and Jenni thought she detected a slight grimace turn down the corners of that steeltrap mouth. Go on, she thought, tight-lipped, tell Paul I'm nothing but a flipping nuisance!

But Ross wasn't rising to the bait. His heavy-lidded gaze slid back to the printed page.

'Seeing you again, Paul, after all these years . . . ' In her affectionate way she reached out and gave the Mission priest's hand a warm and sisterly squeeze. 'Compared to working in a great big London hospital, I think — well, there's a *simplicity* about life here at the Mbusa Wa Bwino I'm already finding deeply satisfying.'

She hurried on earnestly with, 'It's so totally different from anything I've ever known — the experience of a lifetime. Already I'm asking myself if I'll ever want to go back to the UK.' Golden eyes flicked challengingly to the doctor's face.

Only to find herself defying the back of his head and upper torso since he had swivelled round in his chair to hold out his coffee cup for a refill.

Paul gestured to her empty cup. 'More coffee, sweetheart?'

He used to call her that when she was in the sixth form and very reluctantly wore reading glasses. He'd comforted her when some idiot called her 'Four Eyes'.

'No, thanks. I want a really good sleep tonight.'

'Would you mind?' interrupted Ross's deep-toned voice.

'Of course . . . ' she murmured ambiguously, pushing across the table the bowl of brown sugar, thinking yes, go on, take two big spoonfuls to sweeten you up. But immediately she felt contrite, for hadn't he been reasonable company this evening, and shouldn't he be given some credit for that revelation about the *uchavi* incident?

Trouble is, considered Jenni, frowning and perplexed, I just don't know what to make of this man. He hasn't an ounce of charm, and when I thought him a tramp I did a disservice to those 'gentlemen of the road'. But he's certainly got something I'd hesitate to put a label to . . . sex appeal, I suppose, she admitted reluctantly. Mmm, I'd really like to find out more about Dr McDonnell. For starters, how he picked up that trace of an Aussie accent. And what motivates him — *apart* from living for his medicine?

So what's driven Ross McDonnell to the Good Shepherd Mission? Who's he running away from? So many questions I don't know where to start.

'Hear that, Ross?' grinned Paul. He clearly liked and respected his medical colleague. They seemed to have an easy, even jocular relationship. 'Our lass wants her beauty sleep, so none of your Benny Goodman tonight.' He winked at Jenni. 'A *jazz* freak, this chap.'

Just then came a commotion in the entrance and Sylvia Anstey hurried in, a navy cardigan slung across her shoulders and the smell of hospitals clinging to her white uniform. 'Ross?' she called urgently. 'You're needed on the men's ward. Matt's having a spot of trouble with the old man.'

Paul and Ross were on their feet, Ross was stretching as if there were all the time in the world. A few people looked up, but it seemed an emergency was nothing special, and most, after a cursory interest, returned to their games of chess or Scrabble, their magazines or their letters home.

Sylvia's ponytail was collapsing in an

untidy mass of tendrils. She looked flushed and pretty and harassed.

Poor thing, thought Jenni, as disturbing visions of witchcraft abroad in the dark of the night reeled through her overripe imagination. 'Shall I come too?' she offered.

But Sylvia waved the younger nurse aside. 'Don't bother,' she said curtly. 'Just be on time for the morning shift.' Clearly it was Ross she wanted, and Ross on his own.

Quite understandably, Jenni told herself, trying not to feel hurt. Sylvia was tired. And hours of long night stretched ahead. Anyway, she realised on a flash of intuition, they were probably having an affair — bossy doctor and the only white and available nurse on the scene. Sylvia, no doubt, saw a new arrival as competition. *If she only knew! As far as macho man's concerned I'm a member of the 'weaker' sex — he doesn't even see me as attractive,* she thought.

'Paul, could you . . . ?' Sylvia

fluttered her eyelashes. 'There's a language problem.'

Jenni pouted visibly. Ye gods, Paul too! Anstey's man-mad, she told herself.

'Of course.' Paul's response was crisp where Ross's was laconic. 'I'll come immediately.' His arm gripped Jenni's shoulders in a bear-hug and he dropped a kiss on top of her sweet-smelling hair. 'Sleep tight, and God bless,' he said.

Ross had strolled over to the door. He said something to Sylvia, and she cast an anxious backward glance at the freckled redhead.

Hell's bells, Sylvia, you don't have to worry about *me*, muttered Jenni to herself as she followed the trio through the compound at a discreet distance. You're welcome to such a wilful, aggressive fellow. I only wish I dare tell you about me and Paul and set your mind at rest. If I get the chance I'll drop a subtle hint . . .

The others passed through the door

of the hospital, leaving Jenni to make her way alone to her sleeping quarters. In her preoccupied state she was scarcely aware of her surroundings, of the single electric bulbs strung out along a line, making hazy patches of light. She didn't even notice that after the warmth of the common room she was shivering.

Then for an instant the generator faltered — causing Jenni to bite back a shriek. Automatically her arms flew out and her heartbeats drummed a wild tattoo. Gone the rational world of the Mission. She was plunged from her reverie into *usiku* — the mystical, fear-charged blackness of the African night.

No more than a second of sheer blind terror . . .

As the lights flickered back, Jenni for the second time that day sped for dear life across the compound — to the uncertain safety of her room.

\* \* \*

Most Africans lived — as Jenni vaguely recalled from geography lessons back in high school days — in tribal villages, cultivating annual crops on very small plots of poor land. It was one thing being told by Miss Langley on a boring Friday afternoon that African women did all the work — yawn, yawn — and quite another thing to come face to face with reality.

Jenni and Matt, strolling past the village on a rare and precious lunch break, could see the adult men lolling about among the huts in the midday heat. Down by the river in the parched stony fields were the women; toiling away, bashing at the hard ground with a sort of short-handled hoe and digging up what looked like dahlia tubers. 'I'm blowed if I'd stand for it!' exclaimed Jenni, indignant at such unfair division of labour. 'What are they digging up, Matt? And what's that tall plant everyone grows so much of? — how it flourishes in these conditions beats me.'

'Ah can tell you're a city girl,

Tadpole. Don't you recognise maize when you see it? And those are the roots of the cassava plant. Personally Ah don't like it — sweet potatoes are nicer, but maybe they don't do well in these parts. Ah guess down here by the river the soil's better and they can irrigate maize plants. It's quite easy to grow and the birds tend to leave it alone. East Africans are real keen on maize. They make flour from it as well — '

'And it makes a lovely game of hide and seek!' interrupted Jenni, laughingly pointing out some children playing among the tall leafy plants. 'Oh-o — there's one of the mothers telling them to pack it in — what a shame! Phew, here's a bit of shade, Matt, I really must take the weight off my aching feet.'

They munched contentedly at sweet, stubby bananas and home-baked rolls filched from the dining room. Below them, its muddy edges imprinted with a confusion of animal tracks and foot-prints, flowed the sluggish brown river, low between its banks.

'And what work do the boys do when they aren't in school?' demanded Jenni with a frown.

'Don't you ever relax, you belligerent dame!' Matt was leaning back against the tree trunk, eyes closed, hands clasped behind his head. 'Quit agitatin' about the inequality of African women! The boys do their bit too. You must've seen 'em early each morning, driving the village's communal herd of cattle past the Medical Centre and on to the grazing grounds on the far side of the Mbusa Wa Bwini. Hey, don't give all your lunch away!' he protested as a little girl sneaked herself on to Jenni's lap for a cuddle, a piece of banana clutched in her small plump fist. 'These people don't eat in the daytime!'

'Oh, the children must do, surely. Look at this poppet, I could eat *you*, couldn't I, sweetheart?' The child chuckled uncomprehendingly and tried to share her banana with Jenni in return, smearing banana mush all over 'the white one's' face. Jenni just laughed but Matt said, 'Ugh, Ah don't know how you could. C'mon,' he urged with a glance at his watch, 'we better get along back, no rest for the wicked.'

That break by the river was a rare treat. As a general rule each waking hour was crammed to the minute with activity. Grab a meal, get to the ward, rush to a clinic, speed by Red Cross truck to visit the village settlements — don't waste a second, ordered Jenni's feverish conscience. So little time, so much to do. And the doctor's all-seeing eye scrutinising her every move, just waiting for the first sign of weakness, of not being up to the job. Like hell she'd give him the opportunity he itched for!

'Let's clear the floor and have ourselves a disco!' suggested Matt after supper on Saturday night. Too late — Jenni's head was already nodding over the mango pudding.

She had soon discovered that for her,

so newly arrived, it required a killing effort to work efficiently in the tropical heat. And she seemed permanently thirsty — with a thirst even iced drinks couldn't slake. The flies particularly got her down. They were everywhere — a plague.

But Nurse Westcott was not going to show publicly the extent of her fatigue. Not a murmur of complaint should escape her determinedly smiling lips.

Kindly Sister Beatrice, perceiving the glitter of exhaustion in Jenni's newly-hollowed eyes, insisted on Jenni breaking off for the occasional hour or so of breathing space. 'Father Paul will be accusing me of working you into the ground. Now be off with you, out of my sight. Who told you you were indispensable around here?'

Jenni grinned, unabashed. 'Oh, thank you, Bea! Do you think it'd be OK for me to nip across to the school and hand over the letters I was telling you about? The ones from the children in Dad's parish back home, asking for pen-friends? And I have lots of photos too.'

There had been no further mention of her supposed weeks of 'trial'. It appeared to be strictly between the doctor, Father Paul, and the by-nature-rebellious Nurse Westcott.

Not much romance about the whole adventure now. Paul was no longer the lover-boy of a young girl's dreams. In fact he was causing the mature Jenni the occasional nightmare from which she awoke with a start, struggling to remember where she was, and why. Generally it took the form of a harassed and heavily pregnant Jenni, her swollen form draped in a batik-printed *kanga*, surrounded by freckled blond toddlers, all boys and all kicking footballs round the one room of a wattle-and-daub hut, while she struggled to support a wriggling baby on one hip and stir the cooking pot with the other, at the same time trying to discipline children who scarcely knew their father from Adam and who seemed intent on turning their wretched mother's fiery hair grey.

Dear old Paul! Any woman sharing his life would have to accept that she took second place — and Jenni knew she was too volatile to put up with *that*. Perhaps, she found herself pondering, she'd never marry. After all, if in twenty-four years she had never found Paul's equal, then in all probability she never would!

It was at this point, as she lay flat on her back, meditating in a darkness shrouded by mosquito netting, that the image of a tall unshaven tramp figure, leaning bold-eyed and insolent against her door jamb, superimposed itself so remarkably on her inner vision that Jenni sat up, open-mouthed and wide awake, clutching the thin sheet to her throat and quite convinced Ross McDonnell himself was there with her in the room —

What an extraordinary trick of the imagination, when the doctor was the very last person on her mind!

Footsteps were passing her door, muffled voices, Matthew Blamey's and yes, that deeply disturbing voice like a trickle of ice down the channel of her spine. To hear him so close, just when she'd been . . . Jenni swallowed repeatedly, her mouth was so dry.

He must have been called to an emergency.

Sighing, Jenni dropped back on to the pillow and reconsidered her long devotion to her sister's ex-fiancé.

The physical attraction hadn't cooled. No way. The sight of Paul still quickened her heartbeat, though the glossy curls had gone and those handsome features were bearded now, the formidable physique pared to the bone. No indeed, he possessed the fatal attraction of the older man.

And maybe, thought Jenni, sleep far away and her senses alert and wide-awake, maybe that's what I'm suffering from: a *fatal* attraction. And the nightmares are a warning of what my fate would be.

'Saints preserve me!' she exclaimed aloud.

A few feet away on the other side of the thin partition, a sleepy voice complained, 'Wha'ser marrer?'

Stifling her giggles, Jenni rolled over on her front and pulled the pillow over her head. She yawned and her eyelids flickered and closed, the golden lashes feathering her cheeks. There'd be lots of babies, she thought dreamily. He was a physically affectionate and demonstrative man — that was his nature. Time couldn't alter that . . . she drifted back into troubled shallow sleep.

★   ★   ★

Beatrice kept a close watch on Father Paul's little friend during those first couple of weeks. She knew Dr McDonnell considered the demands of bush nursing would be too much for Nurse Westcott. He had stated his views in the privacy of her office, and with grim satisfaction.

'By the way, those eye ointments and drugs in the dispensary — where did they spring from? Worth their weight in gold to me!' he exclaimed with a puzzled frown.

Bea slapped a mug of coffee down in front of him as they sat in her tiny office. 'Where do you think they came from? Blessed St Luke himself dropped them down in answer to your prayers, didn't he?'

Ross scratched his stubbled head. He certainly hadn't brought that lot back from Dar.

'You want to be thankful they didn't all melt on that murder of a bus ride.'

'Hell's bells! You mean? . . . But her case must have weighed a ton. Expensive too — how could she afford it?'

Bea filled him in with the rest of the story, relishing the discomfort on the doctor's unshaven face. 'You don't much care for that young woman, do you?'

'Oh, come on, that's hardly fair,' he protested. 'She seems a competent enough creature.'

Ross's eyes were narrowed slits of conjecture. It was a look that Bea recognised as contributing strongly to the doctor's rather formidable image; the African nurses were very shy of him; they found him awesome — though it was clear he was driven by a deep concern to help their people.

'But why come here, why pick on the Good Shepherd Mission?' His finger stabbed the air. 'Because of Paul, isn't it? She's after him, Sister Bea. Yes, you may well look like that! Going to cause one helluva commotion, isn't it, if that's her game.'

# 5

When possible the medical team held a weekly meeting of senior staff to review the past seven days and plan for the next and keep the bursting hospital diary up to date. Out-patient and 'outreach' clinics, all must be recorded; non-emergencies scheduled for minor surgery; expectant mothers likely to need assisted deliveries to be admitted days in advance and given a well-earned rest from long hours coaxing food crops out of the parched soil.

Someone had to hold the fort while the team gathered in the cramped medical office, and today it was Sister Bea's turn. Sister Judith Mary got called away to a minor crisis on her ward.

'I'm demonstrating to a group of visiting eye surgeons in Dar next Thursday and Friday,' Ross reminded them. 'I see we haven't any deliveries booked in till the following Tuesday. If one of our 'problem' mums decides on an early production, our highly competent Sisters of Mercy will cope just as well as I could. Sylvia, you'll take my ante-natal clinic as usual. Now let's see — '

He tapped his pencil on the wooden table top, leafing back through the diary to see how many of his under-fives clinics the new nurse had helped in. With a specialist nutrition course under her belt Westcott was proving worth her weight in gold. (Ross referred to her in his thoughts as Westcott. Somehow it served to defeminise this disturbingly vivid young woman.)

Recalling his earlier reservations, the doctor was thankful Westcott had settled in with so little flap. Splendid job she was doing too, travelling out to isolated regions to set up and organise new feeding clinics. It had to be admitted, considering her objectively (which was easier when you didn't look

143

at her big bright eyes and bee-stung lips), that she was just as physically tough as she claimed.

But Ross didn't blame himself for having initial doubts about the outspoken Miss Westcott; with a face and figure like that, his reservations about her usefulness had been entirely justified. So what *was* she doing out here? — apart from the obvious!

And another thing, frowned Ross, rubbing his chin. Was it sensible to have Matt always drive her out into the bush? Matt was clearly taken with the redhead and had stopped moping about over Nurse Charming.

Wouldn't it be advisable to have her travel with himself — instead of Sylvia who was badly in need of a decent break. Get her away from Matt . . . and get her away from Paul too, come to that.

The busy nurses were fidgeting on their hard wooden chairs while the doctor pondered over the complications in the diary.

144

'Hmm,' he said suddenly, and lifted his head to look quizzically at Jenni. It hardly seemed fair to burden the girl with extra responsibility, but there was nothing else for it. 'Can I entrust the under-fives clinic to you? With the assistance of SEN Lutu who's familiar with my routine.'

Jenni bridled at his doubtful undertone. With her background and qualifications? If she couldn't handle such a clinic she should be ashamed of herself. 'I should think so,' she replied coolly, making an effort to stem her annoyance.

'No *think* about it, Nurse. Either you can cope or you can't.'

'I can! But perhaps you'd rather change the date so you can do it yourself!' said Jenni huffily, her temper and her colour rising. Ross noted this and his eyebrows drew together in an ominous vee.

'We can't do that,' interrupted Sylvia bossily. 'Getting patients to keep appointments is a problem at the best of times.

145

We try marking their cards with seven strokes to indicate seven days, but either they lose the cards or they can't count or their husbands can't count or no one in the village can count. We can't rearrange clinics at the drop of a hat.'

The office was cramped and airless. Jenni's uniform clung damply to her midriff, and she plucked it away from her sweating body with irritated fingers. She tried to play it cool, and failed. 'You know something, Doctor?' she pointed out sarcastically. 'A pair of willing hands doesn't get a nurse a contract to work out here. It takes specialist qualifications — and a grilling on motivation!'

'Weeding out the idealists!' agreed Sylvia with a nod of the head.

Leaning back in his chair, Ross stared down his arrogant nose at Jenni with her pink face, her dusty bare feet and her coppery hair spilling out from under her cap in damp tendrils. He stunned her with a slow provocative grin. 'And to think I thought you came for love!'

Her fingers dug into her palms. 'And what's that supposed to mean?' she fired back recklessly.

Had they been alone this would have led to a stand-up row in which Jenni would have been obliged to tell the most frightful lies. But Ross, after an astute glance at Sylvia whose face had turned oddly white and set, as if the sight of people arguing made her ill, asked calmly and with a change of tack, 'So, have we dealt with everything for this week?'

Sylvia cleared her throat. 'There's the theatre list — ' she began. Her voice wobbled and immediately Ross got up and gripped her shoulder. Sylvia managed a brave, wan smile.

'We can sort that out later, if you're tired,' he suggested kindly.

Jenni looked on, baffled. Sylvia seemed such a tough nut in the ordinary way! And Ross, she'd have sworn, had all the emotions of a block of granite. But not where each other was concerned, that was for sure!

Jenni checked her fob watch. Just time to grab a sandwich before getting back to the ward: she'd feel more civil with something in her stomach after missing breakfast. And besides, the theatre list was Sylvia's concern.

And thank heaven for that! Her inner eye could just picture it. She grimaced as her sense of humour struggled once more to the surface, bringing with it a vision of Ross . . . yes, Ross the Boss, masked and gowned and backing her up against the wall in that shoebox they called an OR, fixing a gleaming scalpel at her throat and demanding, 'The truth and nothing but the truth, Nurse Westcott!'

Sylvia was welcome to the pleasures of being Ross's theatre nurse. She was much better qualified for it anyway, with a diploma in ophthalmic nursing and considerable theatre experience. Jenni could see this would make an even greater bond between nurse and eye surgeon. But she told herself she didn't envy Sylvia one bit.

'I'll leave you to it,' she said, jumping thankfully to her feet to make good her escape.

But at that moment the door opened and Paul's smiling self came to join them, his head ducking under the low doorway, his piercingly blue eyes moving from face to face and settling in surprise on Sylvia. 'Ross, any chance you could spare young Jenni for a couple of hours?' he asked.

'By all means take her,' said Ross, as if dismissing an unruly pupil from his presence. Jenni glowered at the two men.

'Sylvia?' Paul came further into the room. He was wearing his white cassock and he looked magnificently tall and bronzed. His hair needed scalping again and tantalising twists of silvered-blond feathered the nape of his sunburned neck. In a glance he had taken in his protégée's heightened colour — and Sylvia's contrasting pallor. 'My dear girl,' he exclaimed in obvious and genuine concern, 'you're as white as a sheet! Are you not well?'

Jenni pushed past them and out of the door, leaving Sylvia to bask in all this masculine attention. She leaned her back against the wall and lifted her face to the midday sun, closing her eyes and letting all those hostile emotions drain out of her foolish system. Heat could do very strange things to people. She didn't like herself much today. And she was tired, tired, tired. All the time. So tired. Though she dared not allow a glimpse of such weakness to show.

'Ah, there you are.' She felt Paul take hold of her arm and though it didn't make sense she wanted to shake herself free. She opened her eyes, blinking against the strong light. Looked at him and the world came right again. She smiled with the old affection and said, 'I really should go and help Bea — this feels like playing truant. Where are you taking me?'

'We don't get much time to ourselves, do we, sweetheart? I've fixed it with Bea for you to take an extra-long lunch break.' As she heard this, Jenni's heart skipped a beat. Paul was taking the initiative — they were going to be alone together, just the two of them, how *romantic* . . . he might even be going to propose, she realised, with a shiver of alarm at being plunged so abruptly into the fulfilment of her dreams.

'Look at me,' she protested with a nervous little giggle, 'all untidy and dust all over my feet!' Paul squeezed her roughened hand and swung it high as they marched together across the compound to the dining room.

'I thought we might interrupt Father Thomas with his confirmation class so you could have a chat with the seniors and tell them about the school-children who wrote ours those wonderful letters. Then we could take a stroll down to the village and see old Chief Wamabola — he took a real shine to you, you know.'

'Oh — great.' Jenni swallowed her

disappointment and rushed on, sounding to her own ears like a breathy schoolgirl. 'Thanks for rescuing me back there. Things were getting a bit heavy. Sylvia looks to me as if she doesn't get enough sleep!' she added sarcastically, hopping on one leg to shake a stone out of her shoe. Such a fuss because a nurse was looking a bit pale!

She thought Paul gave her a rather peculiar look. And his voice was reproving as he said, 'Sylvia's not a moaner. She caught malaria very badly when she first came out here and we couldn't persuade her to go home. It flares up from time to time. Ross said he'll check her over. Incidentally, you're taking malaria pills as a matter of routine?'

'Yes, of course,' said Jenni. 'I didn't know about the malaria.' She was genuinely sorry; that was rotten luck and would account for Nurse Anstey's variable moods. 'Poor old Sylvia!' she murmured thoughtfully.

'Hardly *old*,' chided the tall handsome priest, 'she's not even thirty. Whoops, here comes trouble!'

Freed for playtime after eating their lunch, the schoolchildren came pouring out into the compound. A crowd soon surrounded the two adults, pink-palmed hands grabbing at Paul's cassock, piping voices beseeching him to play cricket. 'Father Paul! Father Paul! Come on, come on!' the children shrilled eagerly, till Paul clapped his hands over his ears and promised to give them an hour before sunset so that they could practise before the next match with Daktari Ross and Bwana Matt.

'Ross plays cricket?' questioned Jenni in surprise, setting down the tray of sandwiches and lemonade on the trestle table.

Paul pulled out her chair and waited for her to sit down. 'Didn't you see the match after church? Oh no, of course — you were on nights last weekend.' He prised open a sandwich. 'Peanut butter,

I'd never have guessed. You want to see 'im in action — oh boy, is that doctor a demon fast bowler!'

'Demon McDonnell — most apt.' Jenni beamed at Paul over the rim of her glass.

'And you're as wicked a little lady as ever. To think our most eminent doctor has been saying some highly complimentary things to me about your work — '

For once Jenni's quick wit deserted her. She lapsed into a stunned, if momentary, silence.

★  ★  ★

From the start she had been enchanted by the local children, who were obviously fizzing over with good health and happiness, their faces polished with smiles, well clothed and tidy as they sat on long wooden benches in the Mission school. Their village was one of the few with access to a year-round supply of fresh, uncontaminated water. Later that afternoon Jenni was led in proud procession headed by the Chief (who habitually walked about in a white robe under a black umbrella wearing a pair of Paul's dark glasses) and his elders and accompanied by the skipping children fresh out of school, to admire their electric pump and generator installed through the efforts and fund-raising of Paul and his indefatigable team.

But the overall picture was far bleaker. And the workload was harshly demanding, just as she had been warned it would be. At the same time Jenni was intensely moved to squat in a mud hut among African women and share in the joy of birth. She relished the responsibility of organising talks on nutrition and hygiene in the villages, with the African nurses acting as interpreters, training health workers and birth assistants, prescribing and administering drugs and vaccinations. After all, back home a nurse couldn't even prescribe an aspirin!

In those early weeks by suppertime

Jenni was so weary that she ate like an automaton and would have laid her head on the table and gone to sleep there and then.

Her cheerful smile was the stubborn façade behind which she concealed her exhaustion from the rest of this band of stalwarts. The tropical heat was draining most of her energy.

But it wasn't just the climate, she knew that. If only they had better equipment, drugs, sterile dressing packs — it would make the daily routine so much simpler. Sometimes as she boiled syringes over a makeshift camp fire she would shudder, remembering how in her nice modern NHS hospital back home she had heedlessly tossed disposable syringes into the bin. Here in this primitive and isolated village a clean hypodermic was as precious as gold dust.

No packs of pre-sterilised dressings and instruments in an 'outreach' mission clinic. Everything, from bandages to scalpels, had to be packed just so in the big metal autoclave which to Jenni was a machine out of the Black Museum as it hissed and steamed and rattled and roared. A rattling, hissing monster caged in its own special room and seemingly on the perpetual verge of blowing the Clinic sky-high!

At the end of a twelve-hour working day, Jenni would collapse in the privacy of her room for a precious half-hour before supper. Lying on her bed, dripping with perspiration and dive-bombed by mosquitoes, she could just hear Ross McDonnell's satisfied 'I told you so.'

Oh, the humiliation! if she should be sent slinking home like some whipped dog beaten by Ross's stronger will. 'Physically not up to scratch. There can be no weak links in our chain, Miss Westcott.'

And oh! *disappointment* was too feeble a word to describe her distress if she should be separated from Paul — and all because of another man's dislike. Small wonder Jenni found she was automatically going out of her way to avoid situations where she and the doctor might end up alone together.

Came the day when she realised she'd cracked it. Tired, but not exhausted; grimly satisfied with the day's achievements rather than depressed at so much left undone. Gritty realism taking over from the high hopes that she'd started out with. She had come through the ordeal by heat — and she knew now that she would see out the duration of her contract. No excuse for Demon McDonnell to get rid of her now.

She jumped to her feet and punched the air like a triumphant athlete. She even did a few nifty disco steps. A huge and wonderful relief surged through her. She'd worked right the way through from six-thirty to nightfall; she had showered and changed and she was ready for supper with a huge and healthy appetite even for that gruesome goat stew. And tonight, for the first time, she wouldn't have to disappoint

Matt Blamey with another lame excuse.

Tonight, yes, she *did* feel like disco dancing. As her new friends in Dar-es-Salaam had so confidently forecast — yes, she *was* getting acclimatised, learning to pace herself in the enervating heat.

★  ★  ★

Paul was away at Mission Headquarters in Dar. Ross was not at supper. Nor was Sylvia. No one knew where they had gone, but the Red Cross Land Rover was missing. Jenni pushed speculation about those two from her mind.

As ever, the common-room radio was tuned to the BBC World Service. No one ever seemed to switch the thing off, but Matt had his own cassette recorder, and he cleared a corner of bamboo tables and cane chairs and put on one of his Dire Straits tapes.

When the doctor and nurse arrived, late and dishevelled and demanding food, Jenni pretended not to have noticed, dancing even more vigorously to demonstrate her lack of interest and her abundance of energy. 'This'll show you, Dr Boss!' she muttered beneath her breath, hips gyrating beneath white broderie anglaise skirts, Matt in his cowboy boots a proper John Travolta: only the limited space inhibiting their antics.

'Let's take it outside,' he panted. 'More space out there. I got plenty of batteries. Tadpole, you're the greatest!'

But Jenni protested that she wasn't going to ruin her white skirts in the red dusty compound. Peering through the convenient fronds of a six-foot potted palm, she met Sylvia's staring eye. Ross wasn't talking much; he seemed more interested in his food.

They changed tapes and put on Jenni's favourite, a slow Phil Collins number. She linked graceful arms round Matt's neck and he held her as close as he dared. Sister Judith Mary was waving a hand to the rhythm and saying, 'You young people mustn't overdo it, you know.'

'Your turn next, Sister Ju!' teased Matt. 'It's the heat,' he murmured, rubbing his cheek against the hazy curls drifting over Jenni's ears and shoulders and gleaming like beaten copper in the lamplight. 'We've all got sex on the brain out here. Care to join me in the bushes, Tadpole?'

'Matt!' Stealthy fingers were attempting to prise her white top out of her elastic waistband. Jenni firmly moved his hand to safer ground. 'Don't be silly . . . I say, Matt,' she lowered her voice to a whisper, 'Sylvia and Ross don't look very happy. Do you think they've had a lovers' tiff?'

'Those two?' Matt gave a snort of amusement. 'Y'must be joking!'

Jenni shrugged. Yes, the doctor was a very unlovable man — but maybe love wasn't what Sylvia was after. What Matt had said about the heat . . . after all, those two must get thrown upon each other's company more than somewhat.

Sylvia's pretty face wore a look of weary petulance. She looked as lethargic as Jenni had lately felt. Perhaps it was the malaria again, thought Jenni sympathetically. She found herself envying the experienced older nurse who had proved herself strong and capable — and worthy of the doctor's admiration.

Allowing herself another peep over Matt's shoulder, Jenni felt a certain chagrin. While Sylvia darted bad-tempered glances at the entwined pair, Ross was ignoring them entirely.

Oh hell! thought Jenni, biting her lip. What more can I do to convince her I'm not hankering after her precious doctor? If Sylvia would only keep her eye on her own man, she'd realise he's hardly glanced in my direction since he came in — contrary brute that he is. Just when I want him to notice me he's not interested. Other times he stares as if I'm curiouser than a dinosaur! Can't win, can I, Dr McDonnell?

Another peep seemed permissible.

Ross had fetched coffee for the two of them, and from his pocket was producing a hip flask. Unscrewing its silver cap, he dosed both cups, and Sylvia was smiling at him now. Jenni saw her lay her hand over his, as if to say, no more, that's enough. She wished she were close enough to overhear what they were saying. Ross lifted a hand to Sylvia's hair and tucked an untidy lock behind her left ear. An extraordinary pang pierced Jenni to the heart. From such a man it came as a shock, a rare and tender gesture . . . imagine what it must be like to be on the receiving end of this disturbing doctor's caresses!

Dwelling on this made Jenni's heart beat faster. She was quite taken aback with herself for letting physical attraction get the better of her judgement. After Ross and Sylvia had left she seemed to droop and lose her earlier sparkle.

Matt protested when Jenni sighed and said she had really enjoyed herself, but it was time to turn in. 'I'll walk you back, then. Never know what's out there, lurking in the night.' He laughed when Jenni shivered.

Sylvia's room was in darkness. Either she was in the shower or had already turned in. Or else . . .

Feeling the slight tremor, Matt tightened his arm about her waist. She knew she shouldn't encourage him, he was only a boy really. And it wasn't fair, because of the way she felt about Paul. But when you were lonely and far from home, and Paul wasn't there and —

'Will ya listen to the-at!' exclaimed Matt.

Jenni mimicked his Southern drawl, 'Listen to wh-at?'

They paused on the verandah steps. Lazily, on the smoky night air, throbbed the slow seductive beat of some long-forgotten melody. Jenni began to hum along with it. Were there words? She didn't know them.

'Who's that?' she asked curiously.

'That'll be Ross the Boss loungin' on the verandah and smokin' a mean cigar.

Sometimes you could almost believe that guy's ornery flesh'n blood when he sits outside in the dark and listens to his old jazz music. Reminds me of my pa — he's a Miller fan too.'

'Miller?' wondered Jenni.

'Don't you reckernise Glenn Miller?' Matt grabbed her elbow. 'Come on, li'l lady, 's very appropriate, *Moonglow*.'

Jenni wrenched her arm from his grasp. That comment about Ross reminding this medical student of his father only emphasised Matt's youth and inexperience. Encouraging the crush he was in danger of developing on her would be downright mischievous. She checked her watch. 'Shouldn't you be doing a round right now? Bea'll have your guts for garters!'

Turning the corner, Jenni saw the doctor and smiled to herself. He had set a deckchair and table plonk in the middle of the square. A half-burned candle guttered on the table, and a wind-up gramophone played scratchy records donkey's years old. Ross lay back with his bare legs stretched out and his hands clasped behind his head. His eyes were shut. He hadn't seen her. No cigar. And no Sylvia.

Quietly Jenni opened her door and gathered her washing things. To get to the bathroom she must cross where Ross was sitting, or take the chicken route, creeping round the verandah to escape notice.

The music of *Moonglow* concealed the flip-flap of her espadrilles as wrapped in her black-rose kimono Jenni sauntered past Ross in his deckchair. His back was towards her. Neither acknowledged the other. Sylvia was in the showers. Jenni called out, 'Good night, Sylvia,' and heard the spray switched off, followed by a friendly enough, ''Night, Jen!' that lifted the younger girl's spirits.

Ross's presence had turned a two-minute stroll into a minefield. Typically egotistical to switch off the outside lights and park himself smack in the middle of the open square so one had to weave one's way round him in the darkness. His candle had burned away now to the merest glimmer, but the doctor was so engrossed in his mood music and his reverie that he hadn't noticed. A penny for your thoughts, she'd have liked to offer. Ross drew deeply on his cigar. The glowing point intensified and above it his eyes suddenly glittered in the darkness. The Demon Doctor, thought Jenni with a shiver of fascination.

It was still *Moonglow*; he hadn't changed the record, and the combination of music and starlight was sheer magic. Jenni had the most amusing idea. It came to her out of the blue. Dr Boss seems to need cheering up tonight. I'll ask him to dance with me! Why not? He can only bite my head off! And if he turns me down then I'll know for sure that man is inhuman — for who could resist a waltz beneath the stars on a night such as this?

Hardly dressed for it, are you, you brazen hussy, pointed out the voice of common sense. You haven't even got your knickers on. Remember what Matt said? They're all sex-mad. You'll get thrown into the bushes and —

'Good night, Dr McDonnell,' she murmured as she passed, her eyes demurely downcast, pursing her lips to control the laughter rippling through her voice.

'Ah . . . good night — ' His eyes dwelt on the slender figure, a sylph mingling with the velvety night.

He seemed momentarily to have forgotten who she was, preoccupied by his own deep thoughts. Jenni's mood altered on the instant. Her laughter faded from her lips. She was glad she hadn't intruded with that silly impetuous suggestion. What was it Sister Bea had once said? . . . that she sensed a great unhappiness in Ross's past. At the time, not knowing the man very well and not liking what little she did know, Jenni couldn't have cared tuppence. But now she sensed that he was feeling sad, and she was sorry.

Concealing herself behind one of the wooden posts, Jenni concentrated her compassionate gaze on the lone figure. Cigar smoke spiralled upward through guttering candlelight just to the right of the shadowy head.

Yes, Ross could be rude and impossible and casual; but these in themselves were attractively provoking qualities and set the adrenalin flowing in a most exciting way. And of course, he was an entirely admirable doctor, she reminded herself as she let herself back into her bedroom and prepared to plait her hair in readiness for bed, the only way to tame that riot of curls so that it would be manageable in the early morning. 'My hairbrush!' exclaimed Jenni in annoyance. 'I've left it in the bathroom. Oh, flip!'

She tightened her kimono belt and crept stealthily along the passage. There was no one about. The early-to-beds had been snoring their heads off for hours; the late-birds were still playing Trivial Pursuit in the common-room.

The deckchair was empty and the candle had gone out. The record-player was silent. And Ross was gone.

'Well! How strange.' Jenni folded her arms and shivered. Something wasn't right, something was . . . different. She peered shortsightedly into the dimness as if a clue might lie in the deserted deckchair or the dribble of candlewax.

Her ears proved sharper than her eyes. The music had been replaced by a new and frightening sound, the unmistakable throb of African war-drums, beating in ominous rhythm. And seeming to come from the village down by the river. What could it mean? Should she wake someone? Had Ross gone to investigate, alone, a white man in the mysterious spirit-haunted African night?

Jenni forgot all about her hairbrush. Ross might be in danger! Those drums sounded ominous. There wasn't a moment to waste. She stopped only for the brief moment it took to throw off her wrap and pull on jeans and a sweater before racing out into the compound. Not another soul in sight, no one to raise the alarm. It seemed as if she and Ross were the only ones who had noticed the drumbeats. She had to be quick.

Following the string of naked light-bulbs, she came to the generator and turned left along the path along which early each morning young boys led the village's herd of cattle and goats to the higher pastures beyond the Mission. Now there was no illumination other than the stars, and the thorn bushes scratched her arms and legs if she veered from the track. 'Ross!' called Jenni. 'Ross, are you there? Ross, come back!' She plunged on, too anxious to be frightened for herself — then stopped abruptly at the sight of native huts silhouetted against the light of flickering wood fires not a couple of hundred yards distant.

'Ross!' she called again uncertainly, and this time there was an answering call from somewhere ahead. 'Who's that? Who is it?'

At that moment, just when her heart was gladdened by the sound, from behind a black thicket stepped the tallest, most terrifying figure Jenni had ever seen. Her arms were grabbed and a calloused hand smelling of earth and animals pressed cruelly over her open mouth ready to scream.

Too late. As if she were featherlight Jenni was plucked from the path. And when the doctor himself came strolling out of the village, a puzzled frown on his face, throwing his searching torch-beam in all directions, there was no sign of anyone at all. Just a size four espadrille lying on the dusty track.

# 6

'*Daktari!*' demanded the fearsome stranger, dropping Jenni right way up but still gripping her wrist as if he suspected she'd run for her life if he released her.

'*Daktari!* I'm not the doctor. Do I look as if I'm *daktari?*' In her indignation Jenni sounded a good deal braver than she was actually feeling. 'Ouch! Let go of me! OK.' She repeated the one word that many Africans recognised, 'OK, I won't run. What's your problem? Why do you need *daktari?*'

The flickering light of a makeshift camp fire showed her captor to be a very tall, skeletally-thin African, the red *shuka* of the Masai wrapped around his bony haunches. In spite of his height and erect carriage the Masai's hair was grey, his features strained and hollow with fatigue.

Though her heart was thumping and

her knees quaked, Jenni made an effort to keep her wits about her. The Masai, she knew, were a proud but reserved people. They roamed the bush, wearing these distinctive red *shukas* and armed to the teeth with spears, driving their herds of Boran cattle on long treks to the waterholes. One of the most difficult tasks was to get them to visit the hospital or the outreach clinics and accept medical care for themselves and their children. 'You are ill, *mzee?*' she questioned, addressing him politely and using the term of respect for an old man. 'You need medicine, *mzee?* Er — what's the word for it . . . *dawa? Dawa?*' she urged, concern replacing the fear in her freckled face.

With a nod of his proud head the old man grunted and pushed her towards the fire. For a moment Jenni had a horrible feeling she was going to end up in a native cooking pot, the traditional fate of the missionary. She almost lost her balance when he gave her another little shove of encouragement and she suddenly realised that what she'd taken to be bedding — the bundle of red clothing near the fire — was in fact a body.

She dropped to her knees on the bare soil and feeling her way cautiously discovered the warmth of bone and flesh under her hands.

'*Yoh!*' encouraged her kidnapper, folding up his stick-like legs and squatting on his haunches beside her. At such close quarters the smell of cattle was more pungent than ever.

Jenni helped him to part the folds of red cloth, but it was too dark to see properly.

The old man reached into the fire and picked out a stick which he held aloft like a burning brand. Now Jenni could see pain-glazed eyes and a forehead dewy with chill perspiration: the smooth-skinned features of a handsome young Masai doing his level best not to groan out loud as he lapsed in and out of consciousness.

For a fleeting moment it occurred to

her that this was the most bizarre situation she had ever found herself in! Then, concern for her safety forgotten, she tucked her hair behind her ears and bent low over her patient, testing his breathing against her cheek and feeling expertly for the carotid pulse.

'Respiration shallow . . . heartbeat surprisingly strong,' she muttered aloud, noting the clammy skin and the dilated pupils. 'Seems to be in shock, but I don't — '

At that moment a beam of torchlight illuminated the trio. Jenni flung up an arm to protect her eyes and the old man was on his feet in a flash, spear menacingly poised.

Out of the bushes, her left espadrille in his hand, guided by the light of the wood fire, stepped Ross McDonnell.

Jenni grabbed at the father's robe. '*Daktari!*' she cried out urgently. 'Here is *daktari* — ' she was going to add 'Don't shoot' like in the movies, but Ross had taken in the situation at a glance, and his command of Swahili, though limited, was enough to reassure the Masai, who abandoned his threatening stance.

The doctor crouched down at her side. 'Are you all right?' was the first thing he wanted to know, his mouth close to her ear, his voice urgent with concern but betraying none of the horror that had shaken him to the core when he had seen and identified that shoe.

'Perfectly,' she breathed a sigh of pure relief. 'And boy, am I glad to see you! Can you shine your torch down here, please. I can't see what's wrong, but I think he's got a pain in his stomach.'

Ross squatted down and shone his torch beam on the exposed abdomen. 'Holy smoke!' Jenni's jaw dropped: in all her nursing days she'd never come across anything like it.

'How did this happen, *mzee*?' In his limited Swahili Ross began to question the dignified old Masai, translating as best he could for Jenni's benefit.

Two days ago while the two were hunting deep in the bush, the son had been gored by a rhino, his stomach ripped open so horrifically that the intestines had spilled out. The desperate father had carried out the most ingenious first aid. Fashioning a needle from a sliver of bone and drawing tough cotton threads from his red cloak, he had sewn the edges of the wound together with three crude red loops which had made nurse and doctor exclaim in amazement. Crude they might be, but they had kept him alive . . . so far. Then across thirty miles of bush with his son's semi-conscious body he had struggled to the Mbusa Wa Bwini. Too proud and too shy to demand help at the hospital door, he had lain in wait until, driven by desperation, he had made his 'kidnap' attempt.

Ross rapped out instructions. 'Take my torch. Get Matt to back the Land Rover up as far as he can. Tell two of the African SENs to prepare theatre for immediate surgery. I'll need your help tonight.'

To pinpoint the exact location in her mind, Jenni looked back at the two men kneeling by the camp fire. She saw her arrogant, cold-hearted doctor warming the son's chilly hand between his own and reassuring that admirable father in halting Swahili, '*Mzee*, you have saved your son's life. Be assured you can entrust to him to our care now.'

As she ran through the dark night she could hear the native drums still throbbing, the stamp of dancing feet and voices chanting down in the village. They did not interest her now.

★   ★   ★

Two hours later Matt wheeled their drowsy patient along to the men's ward. Paul and Father Thomas between them had had the devil of a job keeping the old Masai from bursting into the operating theatre to see what was going on. Now it was all over and Jenni was clearing up the aftermath of surgery.

She worked on like a zombie, collecting up empty saline bottles, stacking trays of dirty instruments ready for the autoclave, mopping down the theatre floor. Ross had saved yet another life, but to him that was a matter of routine and nothing out of the ordinary. He didn't appear to know about fatigue. His arteries — Jenni's twitch of a smile turned into a self-pitying yawn — must pump neat adrenalin!

Matt, who was assisting, had whistled at the sight of the old Masai's ingenious repair of his son's dreadful wound. 'Remarkable piece of work,' agreed Ross, removing the red cotton loops and dropping them into a kidney dish. 'Obviously a budding Fellow of the Royal College of Surgeons!'

During the operation he had been specially considerate of his scrub nurse's tiredness and inexperience; encouraging and kind, and not yelling when she handed the wrong instrument, patiently explaining his plan of campaign as he washed out the stomach and inspected the major organs one by one, before tackling the ripped intestines, chatting affably to keep his hollow-eyed assistants wide awake.

'Did you know,' he remarked to Jenni, not looking at her but peering into the operation site as his gloved hands located and examined the liver, 'did you know that these Masai people live on a diet of milk and blood?' Jenni swallowed her disgust and said no, she didn't, but she supposed that since they were continually on the move, driving their herds of cattle to fresh watering-holes, they wouldn't go in for much cooking. *Fresh* blood?' questioned Matt, pushing his green-capped head close to Ross's to get a better view of the patient's spleen.

'No damage here, thank God for that ... Yup, they trap blood from the jugular veins of their cattle in rotation, so I'm told. One might expect to find a high incidence of heart disease among the Masai, but all the exercise they take combats the effects of a high-cholesterol diet. As we can see here, all organs in the pink, and there's no free blood in the peritoneal space. Now, my intention is — scalpel, please, nurse — yes, I'll have a number two — to give the colon a rest by re-routing the faecal stream through the abdominal wall, thus creating a temporary diversion to allow the gastrointestinal tract to heal.'

Matt didn't envy the surgeon the prospect of explaining sophisticated Western surgical techniques to a primitive bushman. 'How you gonna tell these guys?' he queried.

'With difficulty! The aid of diagrams. And Father Thomas translating.'

'The old feller'll be camping out at the bottom of the bed for the next few weeks,' predicted Matt lugubriously. 'Till you put the colostomy back. Sister Bea'll go crazy! Say, Boss, maybe one of this guy's great-grandchildren will be a surgeon too. Could be in the family genes.'

Jenni had blinked and smiled beneath her mask. 'And today's bush children will grow up to be the doctors, priests, teachers and nurses of the future,' she observed with dreamy satisfaction.

Matt's next question had her wide awake, ears flapping.

'How's about sneakin' along to the Chief's birthday party when we get outa here, Boss? Reckon things'll still be swingin'. Oh, man, the rhythm of those native drums really gets to me!'

'Dr Blamey, could you try and keep your head out of my field of vision?' complained the much taller surgeon. 'I took a look-in earlier and paid my respects. And a good job too, since it happened I was within earshot when our excellent theatre nurse decided to take a walk on the wild side. Nurse, have your fingers turned to butter all of a sudden? No, of course I don't want you to pick it up, woman, just give me a replacement.'

Jenni was late for supper. She was waiting for Dr McDonnell, who always insisted on being called to see any child running a temperature.

When he came striding in he found her sitting beside the empty cot, cuddling the listless three-year-old who had been admitted the previous afternoon for observation.

Ross rarely wore his white coat on the ward because he maintained it frightened the children unnecessarily. He looked at the charts and examined the girl's chest and ears and throat, hummed tunelessly as he went down to the dispensary to locate the antibiotic he was prescribing. He patted the damp curls with a cheerful hand, promising, 'She'll be running around by tomorrow,' and requested Jenni's presence at the crack of dawn to accompany him on a long and uncomfortable trek into deep bush country, because Sylvia, his usual nurse, was taking three days' leave, and dammit, she deserved the break. Jenni quite agreed, and endeavoured to conceal her pleasure at the prospect of a whole day with Ross beneath a façade of professional gravity.

They set off next morning after a hasty breakfast.

When the Land Rover was loaded Jenni let Kefa get in first so that if he wished to take the seat next to the driver he could do so. But Kefa climbed into a rear seat and buried his nose in a pharmacology textbook, studying for his next lot of exams.

'What are you waiting for?' questioned Ross impatiently as Jenni hovered with one foot on the running board and an anxious eye scanning the compound.

'Merryjane is supposed to be coming with us today.' Merryjane, one of the African girls trained by the nuns to work in the hospital, had been told by Sister Bea that she must travel with Nurse Jenni and do the translating for her, and she must be sure not to keep Dr Ross waiting first

185

thing in the morning. For some unfathomable reason Merryjane had responded with a fit of the sulks. Jenni had a nasty feeling she wasn't going to turn up.

Kefa looked up and said there was no point waiting for Merryjane. She wouldn't be coming. Evil spirits would get her if she went too far from her village. Anyway, he said, everyone knew she was a lazy good-for-nothing.

This was vexing, but clearly they must leave without the girl. Jenni hoisted herself in beside Ross, who rolled down his window, let out the clutch and reversed out of the shade of the baobab in a flurry of dust.

'I do love the early morning,' said Jenni to calm the atmosphere. 'The skies are such a glorious mix of colours. And it's so wonderfully cool.' She had a navy cardigan draped across her shoulders, and in her pocket an old cricket hat of Paul's, shrunken with laundering, to protect the back of her neck.

'Get out of it!' bawled Ross as one of the village dogs loped across their path.

They were soon heading along flinty murram roads through a landscape of yawning distance, the Land Rover chugging along like a sturdy tug through the grey seas of bush.

In spite of the dust the air was pungent with the spicy smell of African sage. In the far distance hills rose like tombstones, and the sun climbing steadily into the sky glittered on a million cruel thorns. Jenni shivered with a strange excitement. She eyed Ross's hands on the wheel, well-shaped and strong-looking, and yet so sensitive; hands that could work the most delicate miracles of micro-surgery upon damaged eyes.

'Where is it we're heading for?'

'Mji wa Huruma — Village of Mercy, so-called because the people are desperately poor and badly needing help. They have no well and the road's no more than a beaten track, which is why this place has only recently come to light. This'll be my second visit. Sylvia and I came out here three weeks ago.

First chance I've had to get back.' Ross was blatantly eyeing Jenni's exposed thighs where her skirt had rucked up with the swaying of the vehicle. 'They're not used to seeing white women. Lord knows what they'll make of you.'

The truck hit a series of ruts and she was thrown violently against Ross's shoulder. 'Sorry!' she gasped as she pulled herself upright and hung on to the grab bar. 'What a terrible road! This really is the back of beyond!'

'Got possibilities, though,' pointed out her laconic companion, apparently impervious to the discomfort. 'Could be suitable for ranching once they solve the problems of water supply and lack of communications. And — ' he added, wrenching on the wheel to avoid a particularly lethal pothole, 'eliminate that . . . accursed . . . tse-tse fly. But until large sums of money are made . . . available . . . these remote areas will remain backward and undeveloped.'

Jenni was gazing mistily at the huge

skies and the strange wild beauty of the bush. Had this man no soul? Trust an Aussie to want to rip up the bush and criss-cross it with tarmac roads and telephone wires! 'I don't see that our Western way of life is so wonderful we should inflict it on black Africa!' she challenged frostily.

Ross wasn't impressed. 'Let's see if at the end of this day you can look me in the eye and repeat that.'

But Jenni refused to let herself be intimidated. 'It sounds like *Uncle Tom's Cabin* all over again! Who would run your ranches, Dr McDonnell? And who would do the hard graft?' Remembering Kefa, she glanced back across her shoulder, but his book had fallen to the floor and he was sprawled in a doze across the seats.

'Don't be a little fool!' The words were ground out between his teeth, for it was taking all Ross's concentration to keep the truck on course. He was clearly exasperated. 'We don't want to take over! We're teaching them to run their own show. You've heard Paul say he'll pack his bags when the African priests are ready to take charge. The best long-term solution to Africa's problems is to help her to help herself — but it takes *time*, dammit, girl! Europeans have had hundreds of years to build up teaching skills. Skills that can't be acquired overnight.'

The muscles in his forearms stood out rock-solid as he hurled the Land Rover from side to side. 'Why do you think I've come here?' he demanded. 'The most valuable contribution I can make is to teach and demonstrate eye surgery in city hospitals. But at the same time, I have to roll up my sleeves and get out among these people who can't wait till Africa has enough doctors of her own.'

Oh boy! We haven't been on the road five minutes and we're fighting, thought Jenni, her blood stirring with a secret thrill. Life with the ferocious Dr Ross is never boring! I'd better calm him down before he wrecks the truck. Try a change of subject. 'Were you born in Oz?' she asked. 'I can hear it sometimes in the way you say don't or won't. It's those long vowel sounds,' she chirruped brightly.

'Most perceptive of you,' came the dry response. 'No doubt being blind as a bat has sharpened your hearing.'

Jenni opened her mouth to protest indignantly, but was forestalled. 'I've seen you holding record cards six inches from the end of your freckly nose. Too vain to wear reading glasses, eh?' Ross threw back his head with a roar of laughter as Jenni looked haughtily away.

Actually she was pursing her lips to stifle her own laughter; did nothing escape the doctor's eagle eyes?

'Now let's see, you were investigating my background. Well Nurse Westcott, your powers of detection serve you well. Born in Brisbane, yes, thirty-seven years ago. My mother came originally from Ayr in Scotland. My father from the city of Edinburgh, youngest son of a consultant physician at the Royal Infirmary.'

'Was he a doctor too?'

'Nope. An engineer. The only one of the three sons who wasn't interested in a medical career! Soon after they were married, my parents went out to Australia where Dad was working on a hydroelectric project in Queensland. They loved the place so much they stayed.'

Jenni let go of the grab rail and flexed her aching palms. They had arrived at a road junction and Ross pulled up all of a sudden to check his maps. She practically ended up in his lap. 'Gosh, that is interesting,' she gasped, hauling herself back into her seat. 'When did you come back to the UK?'

Ross wasn't wearing shorts today, instead a faded grey bush shirt, sleeves rolled up to the elbow, trousers bleached almost white with laundering. 'After my father died,' he said, 'my mother came home to Ayr and I was sent to Gordonstoun. From there I

192

went to medical school — Edinburgh, naturally.' The quirk of his eyebrow said clearly, 'Satisfied now you've dredged up my life history?'

Jenni wanted to ask why his father had died so young, but didn't like to in case the memory should be upsetting. 'Gordonstoun!' she observed with a grimace of pity for the young Ross. That most rugged of schools where, if her memory served her right, the boys swam in the wintry North Sea and tackled army assault courses before breakfast! 'So life on a mission station could hold no terrors for *you*.'

Ross surveyed his companion with a cool and clinical eye. 'You're not doing so badly yourself, Miss Westcott.'

Jenni decided to take that as a compliment. 'Why, Dr McDonnell, does that mean you're glad you kept me on after all?' she queried with a fine trace of sarcasm.

That very moment they hit a spectacular rut and all four wheels left the ground. Ross gritted his teeth.

'Hold tight! You OK back there, Kefa?'

'OK, Doctor.' Jenni twisted round and bestowed a warm smile on their forgotten companion, now wide awake and struggling to a sitting position. Ross's next remark wiped the smile off her face.

'You seem to have a very strong motivation to stay.' There was a slow deliberation in the way he said it. Jenni knew he had Paul in mind, and that he intended her to know it.

After a momentary hesitation her reply was cool. 'Perhaps we both have.' It was a shot in the dark. But she was watching Ross closely and didn't miss the flicker of muscle in his cheek, the steel in the jawline. Could you be married? she wondered tensely. Thirty-seven. Devilishly attractive. How could you not be . . .

Back home, the wife. Out here, Sylvia. Perhaps Ross was a man with a heavy conscience. For the rest of the journey Jenni was very subdued and thoughtful.

At last, at the end of a long dusty track, they came upon the Village of Mercy, and Jenni forgot her private worries.

At first glimpse the village seemed very picturesque: a cluster of thatched rondavels looking like giant windowless beehives, the doorways specially low and small to discourage malevolent spirits from getting inside. But closer inspection showed a clearing in the bush where pathetic efforts had been made to scratch a few meagre crops out of the thin soil. Several goats were tethered nearby in the shade of a mango tree.

Slowly and suspiciously the village families emerged from their huts to stare at these intruders. They soon recognised the doctor and Kefa and began gesturing with some animation at the Red Cross truck. But at the sight of Jenni they muttered and pointed, even giggled.

Apprehensively she folded a blue headsquare into a triangle and tied it peasant-style to cover her hair.

Jenni was stunned into silence by what she saw. This was Africa at its poorest level. The people wore tribal dress, with bead necklaces and charms designed to ward off evil. The youngest children went naked. Most were undernourished and lethargic, with lustreless eyes and sticklike limbs in contrast to their swollen tummies.

Tears burned in Jenni's eyes at the contrast between these unhealthy mites and the bright, happy children who lived closer to the Mbusa Wa Bwino Mission. It had taken so long to get here: how could a few hours' work do much to help? 'Oh, Ross!' she exclaimed unthinkingly, and the doctor took one look at the welling eyes and said brusquely, 'Pull yourself together, nurse.'

That did the trick. Jenni was galvanised into action. Muttering that Dr McDonnell had no heart, and well aware that he could hear her grumbles, she set about helping him erect an awning attached to the back of the Land Rover so that they could at least conduct examinations in a bit of shade. The dispenser unpacked his drugs supplies and the rest of the equipment, and some of the mothers, remembering from his last visit that *Bwana Mganga* had asked for a fire, soon started one going with a pile of dry sticks on which Jenni set a pan of water to boil for sterilising needles and syringes.

As she leaned over the fire, she felt her skirts tugged up and heard shrill laughter break out behind her. 'Ross!' she called out in alarm.

'Don't panic,' he said with lazy unconcern, 'they don't mean any harm. They want to know if you're freckled all over.'

The women and children closed in a circle round them, their half-naked menfolk at the rear with menacing-looking faces and spears in their hands.

'Usual procedure,' said Ross. 'Identify all diarrhoea cases and pull them out for immediate treatment. Examine the little ones for signs of dehydration. Sylvia started rehydration therapy last time — see how much they've remembered. I'll make a start on the men. *Jambo!*' he greeted the villagers. '*Habari, mzee?*' he questioned an old man waving under his nose an arm still wrapped in weeks-old tattered bandages. Soon there was a queue lining up to be dosed by Kefa with spoonfuls of medicine.

Jenni started with the babies, cradling tiny heads and with gentle fingers testing the fontanels for signs of dehydration, pinching tummies to see if the skin sprang healthily back into place or stayed limp, looking for dry mouths and sunken dry eyes, a child wailing without tears, classic signs of the dehydration caused by gut infections.

'Diarrhoea kills a child every six and a half seconds,' the lecturer at the London School of Medicine and Tropical Hygiene had pronounced grimly. Along with her fellow students Jenni had gasped aloud in horror.

'Bodily fluids drain away and toxins build up. Within a few hours the kidneys fail and the child dies.'

Jenni put the last baby into its mother's outstretched arms. Surprisingly these children were reasonably well — malnourished, certainly, but one visit from the travelling clinic had already had good effect. Sylvia knew her stuff; she was a very experienced nurse. She and Ross were a first-rate team, and Jenni knew how much the doctor must prefer to work with his girlfriend.

In a rash moment a few nights ago Jenni had offered to trim and restyle Sylvia's hair. To her surprise the offer had been accepted, and while Jenni was carefully snipping away, the older nurse had said she would never leave Africa. Thinking immediately of Ross, Jenni had been secretly appalled. That sounded like blackmail! Was Ross supposed to break his Liverpool contract and stay on here?

But Sylvia seemed in the mood for

confession; Jenni only hoped she wouldn't regret her friendliness later. Coming here, Sylvia confided, had been an escape from a hopeless love affair back home with a married man. She had nothing to go back to, she insisted baldly.

'Oh, surely that can't be true!' Jenni had burst out. 'Why, you could get a Sister's post at the Li — at a big hospital, and who knows — ?'

Sylvia had looked at her most strangely, and changed the topic of conversation.

When she had examined all the children and sent to Ross those needing treatment from the doctor, Jenni settled herself cross-legged facing the group of women. She opened the special picture book issued to the nurses and health workers and held it up for all to see, turning the pages slowly. It depicted vividly the signs and symptoms of sickness and diarrhoea, the mother mixing the 'medicine' and giving it to her child, who swiftly recovered.

The treatment was very simple and very special. 'Some consider,' the lecturer had told his rapt class of students, 'that ORT — Oral Rehydration Therapy — is more important even than the discovery of penicillin. A single dose can save a child's life. And yet it is very cheap, and a mother can administer it herself. No need for a nurse or a doctor. It consists of a mixture of three different salts and glucose and it tastes like tears. UNICEF have undertaken to manufacture, promote and distribute rehydration salts all over the world. People are calling ORT the Child Survival Revolution.'

Squatting on the ground among the women, Jenni looked into their eyes and said slowly, 'Watch me. Watch me.' The women responded with strange jabbering. 'I haven't a clue what you're telling me,' smiled Jenni, 'but you're mighty interested, and so you should be. Now here's a foil packet, see how shiny and colourful it is, see the picture of mother and baby . . .

'Tear it open like this — oh, thank you.' Someone had pushed into her lap a metal pot and one of the plastic one-litre measuring jugs from the Mission clinic. This must be the woman singled out by Sylvia to be responsible for storing the packs of rehydration salts in her own hut, and teaching the other mothers how to treat their sick children. Clinic policy was to find and equip someone in every village to be responsible for this.

Jenni picked up and comforted a grizzling toddler who was rubbing his left ear against a bedraggled strip of animal fur tied round his wrist; village medicine, a cure for earache. He lapped up the water she offered, draining the mug of its pleasant, slightly sweet, mildly salty contents. 'That's a good boy,' she crooned, hugging the little mite close.

'How's it going?' murmured a deep voice in her ear, and lifting her face to the sun, Jenni found Ross crouching beside her, resting an arm across her shoulders in a protective gesture. Escaping tendrils of her red-gilt hair tickled his unshaven chin.

They smiled at each other above the curly head of the wide-eyed child. 'Could you take a look at this ear for me?' she asked.

Her uniform was stained and creased. The doctor's bush shirt was damply patched with sweat, his fatigues caked with dust and grime. Trivial matters that these days she never even noticed.

A deep contentment suffused her; with an effort she resisted the urge to press her sunwarmed cheek against his hand.

'For you, my dear,' said Dr Ross gravely, 'anything.'

# 7

Before they left, the thirsty medical team were offered goat's milk to drink from hollowed-out gourds. There were a lot of brown bits floating in Jenni's and the smell was most offputting. But catching Ross's eagle-eyed signal she knew she must force herself to gulp the mucky stuff down. To refuse would be deemed an insult.

Leaving behind a plastic sack of ORT packs and supplies of dried milk, they reloaded the truck and climbed aboard for the long drive back to the Mission. They waved as they left, and the villagers, copying the gesture, waved back. Suddenly a man broke through the throng clutching a live and furiously cackling rooster. He caught up with the slowly moving truck and ran round to Jenni's side, thrusting the flapping and highly indignant bird through the window.

'What's he saying, Kefa, what's he saying?' she asked anxiously. 'What on earth am I supposed to do?'

'You must accept this gift from the Village of Mercy to 'the woman with hair of flames',' explained the dispenser.

'Oh, my g-goodness! Th-thank you.' The man's grinning head disappeared from view, and Jenni found herself hanging on to two scaly yellow legs while the bird bucked and flailed its wings and Ross said for pete's sake wring its neck before he crashed the blasted Land Rover.

Kefa produced a sack from nowhere and deftly stowed the bird inside, where it settled down huffily with the occasional indignant squawk. Jenni said it was Dr McDonnell who deserved presents, not she, and Ross said it was amazing the impression red hair and freckles made on some people.

'My hair isn't red, it's Titian. Titian changes colour from day to day.'

'I'd noticed that,' claimed Ross

surprisingly. 'Sometimes you're an apricot, sometimes a strawberry. We'll have that bird for supper tomorrow done in a spiced coconut sauce.'

'Oh, how could you! I should choke on every mouthful knowing that those people had far greater need of it themselves. No,' said Jenni decisively, 'I shall take the rooster into school and offer it to the headmaster for a project — '

'Cookery project,' suggested the deep laconic tones.

Kefa tittered discreetly behind his hand and Jenni stiffened the Westcott chin in disapproval, pointedly concentrating on the view from her side window. She wasn't a girl to sulk for long. And all through school they'd said she was a dreamer and a chatterbox. If she wasn't chattering she was daydreaming. If she wasn't daydreaming she was — a sudden thought struck her and she voiced her worries aloud.

'I *do* hope they'll remember to boil the river water like I showed them. I wonder if they understood — ?'

Ross curtly interrupted her. 'No good losing sleep over it. We'll come back in two weeks' time and see how things are.'

'Oh dear. Can't we make it *next* week? It seems so important to build on what's been done.'

Ross was trying to concentrate on following the tortuous track through this wilderness of bush. 'I'm in Dar three days next week, operating.'

Jenni knew that the most complicated eye cases were reserved for Ross to deal with *en bloc* in a marathon teaching session. That was that, then. A fortnight it would have to be.

The place was but one among many, yet Jenni couldn't rid her imagination of the plight of the Village of Mercy. 'Sylvia's made an excellent start on rehydration therapy,' she pointed out generously. 'Next time you take a clinic there I hope she'll notice a real improvement in those little ones.'

'I think you should be the one to

come with me,' said Ross. 'Since you've clearly made an impression! Sylvia won't mind. She's got a lot on her plate, what with — ' The rooster squawked agreement, but Ross never finished his sentence, obliged to concentrate instead upon skirting a crater right in their path.

But what about you? mused Jenni speculatively. Wouldn't *you* prefer to work with Sylvia?

'Well,' she responded quietly, 'it's your decision. I'm quite prepared to go where I'm told.' She relaxed against her seat, as far as was possible in the jolting ride. Of course Dr McDonnell wouldn't be a man to confuse work with matters of the heart. He was a dedicated professional, that was plain to see. And if he wanted her working with him, then that was a vote of confidence in someone he had unfairly mistrusted right from the start.

Jenni yawned and sighed, but it was a sigh of contentment. She felt shattered. But it was a warm, satisfying sort of feeling. They had worked nonstop, all three of them: Kefa, patiently repeating over and over again, '*Amatispoona amabilli kathatu ngelange.* Take two teaspoons of this three times a day.'

She turned to smile at the dispenser, nodding off sleepily in the rear of the truck. 'You did a marvellous job, Kefa. You must be quite hoarse — so much talking. Could you understand what they were saying to you?'

'Some,' Kefa admitted with a flash of that shy smile of his. 'But you know, there are two hundred and twenty tribes in East Africa, each with its own language or dialect. It is not always an easy task to make oneself understood.'

'Two hundred and twenty! Heavens to Betsy, I'd no idea . . . '

Jenni lapsed into drowsy silence. Poor old Ross, having to do all the driving, and in such difficult conditions. Jenni did wish she was a competent driver and could offer to take over the wheel and give the doctor a break. He had been on the go since dawn, and nightfall was barely an hour away: it was vital they hit the murram roads before darkness descended with its customary swiftness.

There was an odd sort of taste in her mouth. She was sure it must be the goat's milk. 'Ross?' she queried.

'Uhuh?'

'That drink they gave us. Did yours taste — er — peculiar? Mine had all these brown bits floating about in it.'

The doctor grinned and for a brief moment took his eyes off the twisting track he had been concentrating on so grimly.

'They use manure to make their drinking vessels watertight,' he volunteered in the pleasant tones of one imparting an interesting snippet of information. 'Which accounts for the brown bits.'

Jenni's insides gave a ghastly lurch. 'I'm going to be sick!'

'Not in our Red Cross truck, you're not,' said the doctor unsympathetically.

She glowered and lapsed into an

indignant silence, mentally ordering her stomach to behave. Was this the same man who but a couple of short hours ago had smiled into her eyes, held her in the circle of his arm, his heartbeats reverberating through her ribs?

As the Land Rover bored its relentless path through the bush, Jenni's vivid inner eye replayed in slow-motion Technicolour that interesting tableau.

Anyone glancing at her would assume the nurse was dozing, a hand cupping the pointed chin and half covering her mouth, eyelids lowered in a sweep of golden lashes on sun-speckled skin.

. . . herself with the child, and Ross embracing the two of them in his protective arm. Jenni shivered to recollect how his heartbeats had quickened as she leaned trustingly back against his broad chest. Now why should that have been? — unless, after all, the cool clinical Dr McDonnell was not impervious to Nurse Westcott's fatal charms!

It was so alarmingly exciting to

contemplate that Jenni felt her own heart begin to race and a blush start up her neck and spread to the roots of her hair. Imagine if he had kissed her, then and there, in front of Kefa and the entire population of the Village of Mercy! She knew that instinctively she had wanted him to, but the instinct had been triggered off by those pounding heartbeats pressed against her sweat-soaked back. It was his fault as much as hers. He hadn't been thinking of Sylvia at that moment. And she hadn't been thinking of Paul . . . in fact, Jenni realised ruefully, she hadn't thought of Paul all day. In spite of the fact that she'd come all this way to be with him.

Paul and Ross. Such very different men. The two were like opposite poles of a magnet, and Jenni felt her emotions pulled back and forth between them, both men in their different ways irresistible. Irresistible. And impossible.

Paul, for all his sense of fun, had matured into a lonely monastic figure who, Jenni was slowly coming to the sad conclusion, would never marry. And as for the intriguing, infuriating Ross McDonnell — well, he had someone in his past. And Sylvia, present and future.

They were on to the murram roads now. Ross heaved a sigh of relief and recalled that an African doctor had told him of a black rhino crashing out of the bush and cannoning into a truckful of medical supplies. The Land Rover had been a write-off, and the doctor considered himself fortunate to have escaped with his life.

Ross pulled out a handkerchief and wiped his brow. 'Physical danger is something I'm not used to,' he claimed, 'but it certainly gets the adrenalin flowing once in a while!'

Jenni glanced at him sharply. There was a glint in those eyes that suggested Ross actively enjoyed a touch of the James Bond to liven things up. She'd known he had a tough streak from the moment she set eyes on him. With that stubble and those heavy-lidded watchful eyes he could be mistaken for anything but a doctor. It was ridiculous that she should find him so devastatingly attractive.

The ride was better but far from smooth. The rolling motion of the Land Rover had caused Jenni's skirt to ride way up over her knees.

When it came out of the blue, the stinging slap left a glowing imprint of Ross's hand on bare flesh. Jenni yelped in pain. 'Wh-whatever did you do that for?' she gasped in stammering outrage.

Kefa in the back gripped his seat in fright. One moment they had been travelling in a companionable silence; the next, Dr Ross had slapped the nurse on the leg! Oh my! He rolled his eyes and his mouth worked silently.

Ross pulled into the side and spread his palm. 'Sorry to hit you quite so hard, but take a look at this. I assure you it would have been considerably more painful if this chap had bitten you.' In his hand lay the squashed remains of a large reddish-brown ant.

'A *siafu*!' breathed Kefa. 'Oh yes, the doctor is right, Nurse Jenni. This ant possesses powerful mandibles which bite and burrow into the victim's skin.'

'Here's my torch. Let's see if there's any more of those little devils before we drive on.' A thorough search turned up three more *siafu*. Kefa thought they might have been concealed among the rooster's feathers.

They finished the journey in alert silence.

$$\star \quad \star \quad \star$$

'Dr McDonnell! I have just about had enough. Either that young man goes or I do.'

Ross's eyebrows registered exaggerated alarm. Invitingly he patted the empty seat on his left and set about placating his senior nurse. 'I'm sorry to hear you feel less than charitable towards my prize patient. A good hot meal is what you need, dear lady, and I can heartily recommend this chicken and peanut stew. Pass a plate along, you chaps down there.'

'It's not young Mgulu who's the problem,' pointed out Sylvia, who had returned from a week in London with a soft curly perm that suited her enormously. And an up-to-date make-up kit and enough new clothes to form a bridal trousseau! She looks smashing, thought Jenni, resting her chin on her fist and enviously watching the scene from farther down the long table. Ross can't take his eyes off her. And she's got that special glow of a woman in love. Lucky Sylvia. And unlucky me, to come all this way and discover that my dreams about Paul were . . . well, just dreams . . . and the man I could really fall for isn't up for grabs!

'He's most co-operative, considering his problem,' Sylvia was saying. 'But his dad gets increasingly tiresome — camping out at the end of the bed, tripping everyone up with that spear he refuses to part with, interfering with the treatment. And *terrifying* the rest of our patients! Fond as we've all become of them, it will make life easier when young Mgulu is discharged.'

'We-ell,' considered Ross, rasping the stubble on his unshaven chin, 'the bowel should be pretty well healed by now. He's a strapping feller, I reckon we could risk it. Tomorrow I'll take him into theatre and close the temporary colostomy. Will that make you ladies happy?'

Bea's faded blue eyes smiled back at him. She had a soft spot for Dr Ross, as Jenni well knew. 'We can certainly use the bed, doctor,' she agreed.

'True enough,' said Ross goodhumouredly. 'Can't have my best nurses getting disgruntled, can I? Now, allow me.' He spooned a generous helping of mashed squash on to Bea's plate, Jenni watching his every move with a quiet concentration she was entirely unaware of.

Sylvia folded her napkin and rose to her feet. 'Cataract list tomorrow, Ross,' she said briskly, all her old energy and dedication quite restored. 'I'll go and see to the pre-meds for you. You'll be coming across to do your usual check-up?'

Ross studied the wrist-watch attached to a brawny sunburned forearm. 'Better see my pre-op patients now — before some other emergency crops up!'

'And I'll come too,' said Matt Blamey, keen as ever to shadow the experienced older doctor and learn all he could. Playing gooseberry, if he did but know it, insensitive boy! sighed Jenni to herself.

Leaving Bea in earnest conversation with the schoolteachers, she found a quiet corner to drink her coffee and tuck a cushion in the small of her aching back. Eyes closed, she let her thoughts drift where they pleased. And as usual they pleased to settle on the person of Ross McDonnell. How disappointing that he hadn't wanted to join her for coffee and a chat about the day's work, as he sometimes did. But natural, of course, that he should wish to be with Sylvia now she was back and looking so glam.

A long sigh escaped Jenni's lips. If being in love made Sylvia look that great, why were there dark shadows under Jenni's own eyes, and why did she feel so solemn? She was in love too. It had crept up on her insidiously, and she'd tried so hard not to give in.

The fingers of her right hand closed over her left wrist and rested there. No need to take your own pulse to diagnose you were suffering from lovesickness! Well, it would go away of its own accord. It just had to. She couldn't be doing with falling in love with a man who had no time for her or her freckles or her short-sighted eyes or her wild red hair. A man who liked his women tall and tanned and handsome, with a brisk manner and a tongue to match.

Too restless to settle, she decided to take a stroll round the circumference of the Mission settlement. The darkness would hide her, and she'd be perfectly safe if she didn't venture away from sight and sound of the buildings. Head down, she wandered slowly past Paul's darkened office, scuffing moodily through the dust and deliberately not allowing herself to look at the building where the doctor would be examining his cataract patients.

At this very moment Paul came coasting into the compound on his motorbike, free-wheeling in a wide circle with his engine turned off so as not to disturb the Mission, heading for the Admin block and coming to a halt beside Jenni.

Jenni decided she didn't want to be alone after all. She brightened visibly, but not before her downcast mood had registered with Paul's perceptive blue eyes.

He pulled off his black leather gauntlets and chucked her under the chin. 'Why so glum, chum?' he enquired gently. 'I had a letter from your pa today. Want to come in and read it? He says they're all missing you and looking forward to seeing you at the end of next month.'

'Next month!' Jenni reeled back. If Paul had thrown a bucket of icy water full in her face it could not have been more shocking. Living each day as it came, all her energies concentrated on the here and now, she had given little thought for the passage of time. And Ross would leave before she did! 'But — but — ' she stuttered painfully, 'I didn't realise . . . I'm not nearly ready to go — '

Paul understood her distress. It gripped you like that, did Africa; seeped into your blood till you could live nowhere else but here. It had happened to him. It had happened to Sylvia. 'You go back while you can!' he warned, softening the seriousness in his voice with a chuckle. He gripped her shoulders in a wholehearted embrace, a pang wringing him as he noticed how slight the bones were beneath the soft covering flesh. He didn't often think of Helen now, but for some reason the memory of his ex-fiancée came back with an aching wistfulness for what might have been. Paul pushed it away with practised effort of will, and switched into counselling mode.

'You've got a very important job to return to. And you're especially needed at the Hanoverian because of your training and experience. Same with Ross.' Jenni relaxed and leaned against him, feeling his hand smooth her wayward hair. His voice was so gentle, so reassuring and calm. You couldn't not respond to a man like this.

He talked on, persuasive, reassuring. 'You've both of you done your bit for Africa. McDonnell's a talented and creative man. He knows he must go back to the UK to continue experimenting with new techniques and advances in eye surgery. Besides,' added Paul cunningly, knowing of old how to stoke the blaze and bring the fire back into Jenni's sad eyes, 'it's pretty dreadful here when the rainy season starts. You'd be fed up in no time.'

Jenni had stomped off in a rage and left him to his late supper.

She had avoided the track down to the village, memories of that kidnapping still haunting the night, making her slow thoughtful way round the outskirts of the Mission, trailing between commiphora bushes whose tortured branches snatched at her flowery skirt, snagging threads of her powder-blue cotton sweater as she brushed past the green bayonets of sansevieria.

Faintly there came to her ears, from somewhere within the Mission, the sounds of Ross's jazz music, indecently exuberant, wild and exciting. Music to be carried away by, taken out of yourself. Not suiting her mood at all.

And indeed why should it? Ross didn't care about leaving. Least of all did he care about leaving Jenni Westcott.

'What's more,' complained Jenni aloud, 'he thinks *I* think he's a *terrible* man! And he also thinks I'm nuts about Paul. And Paul doesn't want me to stay here, so it's clear as the nose on my face that he doesn't intend to invite me to be Mrs P. Hume. Which is just as well, since I find I'm not in love with him after all, and I couldn't marry anyone I wasn't head over heels for . . .

'Perhaps God wants me to be a nun!' she speculated interestedly. 'Perhaps this moment is a turning point in my life and I'm getting The Call.' Carried away by sheer imagination and her own strong sense of drama, Jenni lifted her overawed face to the pale light of the sickle moon. 'Do you want me to take the veil, O Lord?' she intoned in a churchy voice. 'Am I to go into a convent?'

'Sounds a bit drastic,' drawled a voice from behind her. 'What's brought this on all of a sudden?'

Jenni stood rooted to the spot. She'd have bitten out her tongue rather than have Ross McDonnell overhear her dramatic posturing. 'None of your business,' she stuttered, 'I — er — I was just remembering some lines from a play I was in at school. *Heloise and Abelard* — that was it,' she plunged on inventively.

Ross came closer and oh, heaven! he put an arm around her and turned her to face him, lifting her chin so that the moonlight painted her pouting features and closed eyelids. He was so tall — too tall. Jenni automatically raised herself on tiptoe in certain anticipation of what was to come. Ross had both arms round her now, and his face came down to hers, blocking out the moon's magic. Her left arm sneaked up and round to the nape of his neck, her right arm slid under his and clasped that broad, hard-muscled back, feeling the heat of his body beneath her spread fingers. Jenni's only conscious thought was what the hell, it may be the only chance you get, girl, so make the most of it!

Ross laughed a deep throaty chuckle at such willing compliancy and proceeded to take thorough and protracted advantage.

Now there wasn't a rational thought left in Jenni's head. She was vaguely conscious of seeing stars, but they had a peculiar floating quality and she couldn't have told whether they existed within her dizzy head or for real in the velvet-black sky. She'd been kissed many times before, but never with such devastating effect. Her heartbeats throbbed like the native drums. Her body strained to get ever more impossibly close to this man who fascinated and confused her. She put all she'd got into this momentous kiss — incredulous that her old tormentor seemed equally enthusiastic!

At length, when the need to breathe became life-threatening, he relaxed hold of her and after a lung-filling inhalation of $CO_2$ observed teasingly, 'Some nun you'd make! I doubt if a girl like you's still got the basic qualification.'

'Indeed I do have! I've been saving myself for the right man — '

'And you knew you'd find him here?'

interrupted Ross with dangerous quietness.

He had been watching from the dispensary window, had seen her marching moodily off into the night. Lately he was experiencing a new unease about Jenni Westcott. What had happened to the sunny, self-possessed nurse whose delicious appearance had filled him with all sorts of reservations when she arrived at the Mbusa Wa Bwino, simply throbbing with Good Intention? Lately there'd been fewer smiles, and in her eloquent eyes he had recognised a new and grave maturity which only Africa could have put there. And a sadness, speculated the doctor, as she realised Paul Hume was never going to propose marriage.

Experience had turned Ross into a cynical man. Love hurts, doesn't it, Miss Westcott! he mused with chill sympathy. Believe me, I should know.

She'd probably always been the one to love and leave. A girl so appealing would not be accustomed to rejection.

Back in his quarters Ross had reluctantly switched off one of Sydney Bechet's greatest jazz tracks and decided he'd better trail this reckless young woman. At the best of times she seemed to lack a proper sense of self-preservation.

Jenni stepped back from him, her silence mutinous. He was right, and yet unbearably wrong. Much as she longed to tell him she loved him, pride and common sense would not set her tongue free. Not when he was amusing himself with her in a moment of rare boredom.

Ross felt suddenly angry with this tough-acting girl for being so vulnerable. So her frivolous reason for coming to Tanzania had gone wrong, and she was disheartened. So Matt's adoration was no compensation. So she wanted only Paul. Spoiled little brat!

Anger flared and Ross's hand lashed out and gripped her upper arm, the fingers pressing flesh against bone. He shook her to make her answer him.

There must have been many other men in her life: why mope around for the one man she couldn't have? *He'd* be quite prepared to take her mind off Paul, make himself a substitute for the love she couldn't have.

The hell I will! Ross glowered, and set his jaw. I come first with a woman or not at all. He shook her again so violently Jenni almost bit her tongue. 'Let go of me!' she spat, her temper leaping into force nine. 'You're contemptible, Ross McDonnell! I shall be thankful when you're gone from here. Go and make love to your Sylvia!'

'Whoops!' exclaimed Ross. 'My wife would have something to say about that . . . '

# 8

*Running Wild* was the name of the Bechet track, and running wild was the way she'd bolted from him. Ross's amused gaze tracked her till he was quite sure she was making for the safety of the Mission. Then he began to follow at a leisurely stroll. Who would have believed she'd be so devastated to discover he had been married? And as for Jenni's exotic imagination linking him with Sylvia Anstey . . .

A grin spread over the sardonic features. He'd guessed the winsome Miss Westcott was short-sighted, but this was ridiculous. Could she really still be in the dark about Sylvia's romantic inclination?

Yes, technically he was married. But Stef had swept him out of her life. He'd never trust a woman again — especially that wayward redhead with the hot imagination.

Ross strolled round to the far side of the Clinic and leaned against the verandah outside the children's ward. No bleeps in this other primitive world. He didn't like to stray too far out of sight and sound of the hospital knowing that at any time he might be called.

Since he had come to Africa whole days would pass when he didn't think about Stef. That was a definite improvement. He could guess what she'd say about his making love to another woman! She wouldn't give a damn; she'd be relieved. Probably start watching the letterbox for the divorce papers to plop on to the mat. He'd vowed bitterly that he would never set her free to marry that ass Ryman. And he'd honestly believed he would never change his mind, or love another woman. He'd believed himself too single-minded to be at risk. After all, wasn't that why Stef had left him? A four-year marriage to a workaholic surgeon seemed to her no marriage at all.

Breathlessly, in the safety of her room, Jenni was chiding herself for being no end of a fool. But the man was so physically compelling that even a sensible girl like *she* was supposed to be couldn't resist him. She'd joined in the action as if she was his number one fan! Jenni groaned aloud to think of it.

In the speckled mirror she gasped at the sight of her face, the delicate skin all red and chafed from his harsh stubble. Hypnotised by her reflection, she traced with her fingertips the places where Ross's mouth had been and her colour deepened to a glowing crimson. Hadn't she suspected there was a wife some-where? And what about poor Sylvia? The no-good, heartless philanderer!

★  ★  ★

Sunday mornings brought not just the nearby villagers but families in a colourful array of tribal robes and

Western dress, converging on the Mbusa Wa Bwino from all parts of the surrounding bush. The little church could not hold them all, so an exuberant African Mass was celebrated outside in the sunshine.

This joyful occasion formed the high spot of everyone's week, with much clapping and chanting and swaying to the rhythm of maraccas and leopardskin drums, children's voices shrilling above the chanting of the adults, a moment of reverent near-silence broken by the crying of babies.

And afterwards the thwack of leather on wood as a cricket match in the compound got under way, Dr Ross and Father Thomas each captaining his high-spirited team of players to the applause or groans of their enthusiastic crowd of supporters.

Jenni liked to sit in the shade of the church door, a thick quarto pad on her knee and a stick of charcoal smudging her busy fingers. A loving huddle of heavy-breathing children leaned against her chair, affectionately stroking her hair, tugging the yellow folds of the native *kanga* she proudly donned for an off-duty Sunday, fascinated by the magic of her swift sketches.

'I plait your hair for you, Jennee? My turn today — you promised, Jennee,' wheedled a teenage girl wearing one of the white SCF T-shirts Paul had brought back from his last trip to Dar.

Jenni goodnaturedly submitted to having her Titian locks painfully transformed into a halo of small plaits. She was trying to draw one of the village elders, a gaunt-featured grandfather smoking an aluminium pipe made out of a twist of metal off an old Land Rover, tobacco ash sprinkling the front of his best Sunday robe.

'I'm not very good at faces,' she explained when all the little ones pleaded, 'Draw me, Jenn-ee, draw me next!' And her glances would irresistibly stray to the man she had been avoiding eye-contact with since the night of that revelation, her ears finely tuned to the wavelength of his voice. 'Try pitching him a few on the leg-stump,' he was exhorting his bowler. Then, 'Good grief — he's going to knock the ball out of shape!' after a spectacular hit by N'gambo.

Paul was umpire, running a joky commentary on the home-made voice-trumpet Jenni had fashioned out of a rolled triangle of cardboard sneaked from one of the many boxes of candles stored in readiness for when the generator failed. 'And now we've got Father Thomas dancing down the wicket to drive the slow bowler back over his head for . . . yes, it's a straight six — and my goodness, I'd better move that Land Rover before Father Thomas does any more damage!' Cheers from the crowd and a roar as the stumps flew and Father Thomas, his splendid teeth flashing in a broad white grin, handed over the one precious cricket bat to a skinny eleven-year-old in a check shirt and grey shorts a size too big.

Jenni peeped back at her favourite

sketch, drawn soon after she had arrived at the Mission: it was of Ross, seated on the edge of a wooden chair outside the Clinic entrance, wearing nothing but a pair of shorts; his tanned giant legs splayed wide to accommodate a fascinated small boy who was holding up a mirror for the doctor to see his own reflection as he shaved in honour of Sunday.

Ten more days! Jenni shivered beneath the hot sun and her charcoal stick trembled in mid-air. 'Hold still, miss!' protested her hairdresser. Ten more days and Ross would be gone. Impossible to imagine the Clinic without him.

But an African doctor, trained at the Royal Free Hospital in London and with several years' general experience under his belt, was coming to take permanent charge of all medical work.

That night after supper doctor and Mission priest smoked cigars together in a rare moment of quiet companionship. Jenni curled up in a wicker chair with a Reader's Digest in her lap, almost hidden behind one of the ceiling-high Kentia palms. She over-heard Ross remark to Paul that working here in the bush had been the finest experience of his life. Superb training for coping with *anything*, Ross had added with a wry grin, tapping cigar ash into the potted palm and narrowly missing an eaves-dropping ear.

'But as you well know, Paul — because you and I have attempted to thrash this one out before — introducing Western medicine is bound to affect the African culture. Therefore,' the forceful voice continued, 'it's profoundly important that European doctors and nurses are aware of the implications.'

Jenni pulled a face and wished she had a better view of these two splendidly tall and charismatic men, so similarly dressed in their jeans and dark sweaters, so different in temperament and personal style.

'Oh yes, it's all very creditable coming out here teaching basic health education and hygiene, improved nutrition, the importance of clean drinking water and family planning. No, hold on, Paul! Let me get this off my chest . . .

'*Apparently* beneficial — and all credit to Jenni and Sylvia and all of us for working all the hours God sends. We would insist most indignantly that we haven't come here to bulldoze over all those native customs and traditions and 'change' the face of Africa! Yet without realising it we may be doing exactly that!' With his cigar the doctor stabbed the air in emphasis. 'I'm mighty relieved James Matayo is coming to take my place. He'll do a far better job and with greater sensitivity than *I*, with the best will in the world, can ever hope to.'

Jenni was intensely interested to hear this. Ross's reasons for coming here to Africa — and his reasons for leaving — were less puzzling now. He had done his bit to relieve human suffering, taught his specialist skills to more inexperienced surgeons, and now must leave before his own enthusiasm for medicine sought to change a way of life that must be preserved intact.

'You're preaching to the converted, Ross!' The priest had been listening with close and sympathetic attention, long fingers massaging bearded chin. Now he was nodding his head in total agreement. 'That's why I held out for a long-term appointment, and an African doctor as the *sine qua non*.' He gave a short laugh. 'Next one to go will be me, Ross. I am dispensable, and for all the reasons you quote. I shall be replaced within the next couple of years — and by a local man. Father Thomas? No, I think not. He's a good fellow, but the Bishop wants him to take over a smaller set-up.'

There was a pause and the rattle of coffee cups being replaced in saucers. Then Ross's voice again, pitched low and private. 'What will you do, Paul? Go back to the UK once you're married?'

Behind the potted palm a Reader's Digest hit the floor with a gasp and a muffled thud. Jenni froze to stone and completely missed Paul's reply. Ross's astonishing question blocked her ears to all other sound but the confident *once you're married*!

Dizzily she leaned down to retrieve her reading matter. A thousand bees buzzed inside her skull, then all of a sudden turned into butterflies which tickled the back of her throat before fluttering down to her stomach, leaving her queasy with shock.

Paul's intention must be to pop the question just before she left for London! It would have to be very quietly done. He wouldn't want to make a big scene of it, dear Paul, and he'd be well aware that one look at her ecstatic face and the Mission workers would guess his time here was coming to an end.

With such a heavy weight on her mind, Jenni needed to be alone. She pleaded an early night and simulated a hippopotamus yawn.

By skulking behind a parked Land

Rover she managed to avoid Matt Blamey as he came whistling out of the Clinic carrying a torch and a sheaf of papers. Matt would urge her to stay up late, and Jenni just didn't want to get involved in an argument and hurt his feelings with her indifference.

As soon as Matt was out of sight she sped to her room while the coast was clear.

As she rubbed moisturiser into her face and set about undoing all those plaits in readiness for the early morning start, strangely it wasn't her future husband who dominated her thoughts but the steel-spined Ross McDonnell with his uncompromising manner and heavy-lidded all-seeing stare.

Jenni wouldn't have admitted it to anyone, but he'd scared her from the first. Good-looking house-men with smooth manners and predictable lines in chat — that was what she'd been used to and that was what she could handle with one arm tied behind her back. Dr McDonnell was a very different proposition.

You needed to be pretty grown-up to dare tangle with a man like that! sighed Jenni, brushing her hair till it frizzed about her troubled head in a great bush of tiny waves. I wonder what his wife is like?

She swallowed her malaria tablet, then slithered between coarse linen sheets and rearranged the mosquito netting so there were no gaps.

Spreading her hair out on the pillow, she hoped it would calm itself down before morning — along with her pounding heartbeat. Well, she hadn't given Ross's secret away. It was none of her business if he chose to conceal a fact which put him on a whole new unattainable plane.

No, Jenni was more concerned with her own secret and how much of that she had inadvertently revealed in Ross's arms. Poor Sylvia! One consolation — she was no mouse and certainly old enough to look after herself.

Jenni rolled on to her back and stared

at the ceiling, willing back the way she used to feel about her sister's ex-fiancé.

'As for me and Paul . . . ' she confided to the whispery darkness, 'well, it's come as a bit of a shock. I mean, I'd stopped hoping. It didn't seem meant to be. Once I get used to the idea again I know I'll be truly happy.'

She bit her lip, fearful of revealing her precious secret to the listening night. Hell's teeth, she just had to confide in *someone*! 'It's just that I fell rather headily in love with Ross McDonnell and I'm afraid it's — ' a little breathy giggle at her own diagnosis, 'given me a sort of emotional concussion so that I'm feeling kind of numb. Don't get me wrong, though!' Her two hands thrust into her hair as she struggled to convince herself, 'Being in love with Ross isn't at all the same thing as loving Paul. *In love* . . . that's just a horrifically inappropriate crush on someone. Loving means true caring. So just give me time and I'll get over this numb feeling and

243

be absolutely (yawn) deliriously (yawn) happy . . . '

And unaware that delirious happiness was not yet to come her way. Jenni drifted into welcome sleep.

★   ★   ★

'Ouch!' muttered Paul, swatting at his left thigh.

'What is it?' questioned Jenni, leaning forward to get a better look at the crushed remains in his palm.

'Tch, tch! Blue-bodied wasp. Nasty,' diagnosed the knowledgeable Sylvia.

The two girls cooed over his bare brown leg. For nurses, they were unusually sympathetic. 'There's a nasty red lump coming up. I bet that's painful. Ross, I think you ought to take a look at this.'

Paul would have none of it. 'No! I've had painful experience of a good many bites over the years, and survived 'em all.'

'Perhaps you should wear trousers

more often,' suggested Jenni, thinking what a shame to cover up such a splendid pair of legs.

'In this climate? I couldn't stand it.'

Sylvia was sewing a button on Matt's shirt while Matt lounged bare-chested, his jeaned legs stuck up on a chair, slurping Coke from a refrigerated can. She put down her needle and prodded the angry red spot with a dubious forefinger. 'I think I'll pop across to the dispensary and get you something for that.'

'Woman, don't fuss!' Paul protested in tones of mild exasperation.

'Someone out here for you, Father,' called Sister Bea from the door.

'I'm coming.' The eyes of the two nurses followed as he limped out to see who wanted him. Though neither of them said anything, their looks were admiring. Paul had such a splendid build, and his legs were the legs of a tennis player. He preferred shorts for comfort and certainly not from vanity.

Ross McDonnell noted all this from

behind his copy of the BMJ. He had been sitting right beside Paul — and years of clinical experience had shown him something that gave cause for concern. Late that evening he collared the Mission priest, burning the midnight oil in his office.

'How long,' he asked, 'since you had a thorough medical?'

'Good lord, Ross, what a question!' Paul ran a hand over his shorn head. 'I don't know . . . before I came out to Africa, I guess. I haven't had time to be ill. Why ever do you ask?'

Next morning Jenni was surprised when Paul presented himself in the clinic for a medical. In the treatment room Ross gave him a thorough going over. Jenni, bringing in a tray of elevenses, smiled broadly to hear the doctor's verdict. 'All in all, old chap, you're remarkably fit. But I want you to let me remove that blemish above your right knee.'

The cups rattled on the coffee tray. With dread premonition Jenni read the doctor's mind. He suspected a skin cancer! While she and Sylvia were fussing over that wretched wasp sting, now no more than a scarlet pinprick, the hawk-eyed doctor had seen something far more important — potentially life-threatening — and was wasting no time in dealing with it.

'That?' Paul shrugged carelessly. He was a busy man, too busy to notice or to care about trivialities.

They all peered at the mark. Jenni was trembling. She saw a speckled brownish blotch about the size of a half-penny, with a jagged irregular outline. 'D-does it itch?' she asked anxiously.

'No — yes, I think it may have . . . why?' Paul looked up into the two concerned faces. Jenni, bless her heart, seemed on the verge of tears! Genuinely puzzled, he turned questioningly to Ross, who patted his shoulder and handed him his coffee.

'Nothing to get steamed up about, old chap,' he said kindly. Old chap, he kept calling Paul, thought Jenni wretch-edly. Ross sounded genuinely concerned. But he couldn't be, could he? He had no heart.

Ross was thinking quickly. Back in the UK, skin cancer and the dangers of sunbathing had lately received a lot of publicity. Paul probably knew nothing of this. That little growth on his knee had very likely been produced by the sun's rays. Running around in shorts all day gave the sun plenty of chance to do what it liked to a fair Anglo-Saxon skin. Paul was just the type to be at risk. And so was Jenni Westcott with her fiery hair and delicate milky skin.

Ross's head swung towards the nurse, noting the pallor beneath the freckles and judging the girl too emotionally involved for rational thought. No need for panic, silly girl.

The doctor explained. Paul looked stunned. Ross said he would remove the growth, and that once he had done so all should be well. But, he warned, Paul should be on the look-out for further blemishes that might develop in future.

'When do you want to operate?' asked Paul, astonished rather than perturbed by the speed of it all.

Ross checked his watch. 'Anything you can't cancel this afternoon?'

Paul thought for a moment, then shook his head. 'I guess not.'

'You want to help,' Ross asked Jenni, 'or shall I ask Sylvia?' When Jenni bravely said she would scrub, Ross was relieved. The last thing he wanted was to tell Sylvia until all was satisfactorily over.

'Let's keep this between the three of us, eh?' he suggested. 'It's just a minor op. No need to put the Mission in a panic.'

So after lunch Paul went straight into theatre and Ross injected a local anaesthetic. 'Hope that stuff works,' their patient joked as Jenni handed Ross the scalpel.

'Do let me know if it doesn't,' murmured Ross with a pleasant grin, setting the seal on an atmosphere which was lighthearted and far from dramatic.

In no time Ross had excised a boat-shaped piece of skin which included the tumour, and was putting in a few neat stitches.

Jenni covered the wound with a plaster and it was all over. She felt a debt of gratitude towards Ross out of all proportion to the simple technicality he had performed. If Ross hadn't noticed that one small blemish . . . but thank God that he had.

'I'll change into my cassock,' said Paul, pleased as Punch now it was all over, 'then no one will notice anything amiss. There's a week's post waiting to be dealt with in the office.' He shook his surgeon by the hand. 'A thousand thanks, my friend.'

He walked gingerly to the door, turned back for a moment and included nurse and doctor in one of those smiles that melted Jenni's heart. Such a precious, gentle man.

She sought refuge in work, busily

clearing away instruments and preparing the theatre for its next use. 'I'll just take these to be sterilised,' she said in a very small voice, quite unlike her vivacious self.

Ross eyed the ashen-faced nurse with sympathy. The last couple of hours must have held a special torment for Jenni Westcott. He stripped off his surgical gloves, and as she waited to take and dispose of them, he touched her wobbly chin with a questing finger. Smile for me, he wanted to demand of her, selfishly, and his touch left a trace of powder from the inside of his glove, scarcely whiter than her pallor.

'All over,' said Ross softly. 'Nothing to worry about now, eh?'

His unexpected tenderness was more than she could bear. She picked up the tray of instruments and fled to the autoclave in its monstrous den, loading the thing willy-nilly, slamming the lid shut and sheltering there while the steam poured in and the great metal tub rattled and rolled and she indulged in a good cry with a pillowcase for a handkerchief.

Ross was angry. He strode round the wards like a bear with a sore head, then shut himself in the office to write up some notes. But he couldn't concentrate. Her distress was hurting *him*. It was written all over the girl's face that the love of her life was Paul. His *little sister* indeed! That girl was nobody's little sister. She was, every inch of her, a mature desirable woman and just what the doctor would have ordered for himself.

Why the hell did those two have to keep their engagement such a deadly secret? Surely they could let the senior staff in on their plans.

I can't tell her! Ross fumed, stabbing a full stop and making an ink stain explode across the paper. Why didn't Biros last five minutes in this heat? Where in hell did Bea hide the blotting paper? He started slamming drawers and swearing.

He was the very last man ... she

didn't trust him, would entirely misunderstand his motive.

I just hope I'm gone before she finds out, that's all. I'm the last person she'd turn to for comfort. And I don't want to get involved with a woman ever again. Not even my tempestuous Jenni, who's looking for a ring on her finger and a lacy bridal veil to cover her beautiful head as she trots down the aisle of her father's church. Just as well I leave at the end of the month. I couldn't comfort her when —

There was a knock on the door and a flushed face framed by steam-damp tendrils looked into the office. Jenni smiled at Ross rather sheepishly, love and gratitude blazing from red-rimmed eyes. In the space of a blink it was gone and Ross knew that he must have dreamt it. 'Sorry, doctor, you're obviously busy — '

She looked better already. Ross spread his hands and grimaced craftily. 'Don't know where Bea keeps the blotch, do you? I'm getting myself in a mess here.'

'In that bottom drawer. I'll find it for you. If I can just squeeze past — oh, sorry.'

Ross swivelled his legs round to let her into the cramped space and with a catch of breath Jenni felt his two hands helpfully circle her narrow waist.

At this interesting moment Sylvia appeared at the door. 'What's going on?' she demanded.

Ross signalled to Jenni with his eyebrows. She forgot the blotting paper, muttered an awkward excuse about measuring the milk powder for the babies' feeds, and made herself scarce. How unfortunate! She did hope Sylvia wouldn't misunderstand.

One of the African SENs had seen Father Paul coming gingerly out of theatre with a bandage on his leg and looking distinctly dazed. Sylvia, on hearing this, had come pell-mell in search of Ross. 'Look here, Ross, what's going on?' she demanded, at this stage more curious than worried.

Ross put an arm round her shoulders and pulled the tall girl close to his side. Jenni hurried back to the wards, knowing they'd be short-handed without her.

In the daytime heat some of the beds were wheeled out on to the sheltered verandah and in one of these lay an old woman, shrunken to skin and bone and dying of TB. She called out for water and Jenni, with a hundred and one jobs awaiting her, quietly held the skeleton hand until an anxious blue-uniformed enrolled nurse requested help with the naso-gastrically fed babies.

In her tea-break, to ease her mind, she planned to slip across to the office to see how Paul's leg was. She was just leaving the building when Matt sprang out of nowhere and excitedly grabbed her by both arms, twirling her round and round in an impromptu dance.

'What's brought this on?' asked Jenni, forcing her solemn face into a smile for her exultant friend.

Matt's tartan shirt was half unbut-toned, revealing a V of glossy black curls and a white envelope stuffed alongside. The paper crackled as he clasped a dramatic hand over his heart. 'Such a letter Ah've had! Hey, Tad-pole — ' he jerked his head in a sudden double-take, 'look at you! An' your hair all mussed up like that. Have Ah missed an emergency?'

Jenni glanced down and saw she was still wearing her green theatre dress. Bemused with concern for Paul she'd forgotten to change — and not a soul had commented! 'Oh, this. I — I was sterilising some dressings. The steam ruined my hair-do.'

'No surgery was scheduled!' Matt wasn't to be put off the scent so easily. 'Paul loaned me his *picki-picki* to take supplies along to one of the villages. Ah wouldn'a gone if Ah'd thought — '

Jenni interrupted with a rush and an over-bright smile. 'Now what's this exciting news you came to tell me?' she probed, tucking a small roughened

256

hand into the crook of Matt's elbow. 'Tell me quick, my tea-break's nearly gone and I have to change.'

Producing his letter like a proud conjuror, Matt explained with totally disarming eagerness that he'd come to tell her first, because he just *knew* Jenni would be pleased for him. And while she chided herself for a misery-guts, Jenni's tense face softened with real affection for the young American. If it hadn't been for Matt's companionship in the early days, she'd never have survived the ordeal of Ross McDonnell's hostility.

He stamped his cowboy heels and if he'd had a hat to match he'd have flung it sky-high. 'Charmin's coming back!' he announced.

'Charming?' she queried.

'Yup, Charmin'. Ain't that great? She's passed her Midder exams — that's deliverin' babies, y'know — '

Jenni smiled. 'I do know.'

'So she's leavin' the big hospital in Moshi and comin' back to the Good

Shepherd to work. That means I'll get to see her before I leave for Alabama. Ain't that the most sensational news, Tadpole? C'mon, Ah'll tell you all about me an' her while you change. See, we've had to be careful. Her daddy's a bishop and he won't rightly care for Charmin' goin' with a white boy.'

He shoved a dog-eared snapshot six inches from Jenni's dazed eyeballs. 'Goodness,' she murmured, 'what a happy-looking girl!' She shook her head, bemused. Why hadn't Matt mentioned this nurse, this bishop's daughter, this Charming, before?

One thing Jenni *was* sure of in her own mind: after the fright Paul had given her today, she could bear the tension and uncertainty not a moment longer. The first chance they got to be alone together, she and Paul were going to have a very serious talk.

In the glorified broom-cupboard which served as nurses' changing room Jenni pulled off her theatre gown. The young American leaned on the wall outside, gazing at his photo and continuing the conversation through an inch of open door. What a little beauty! What a lovely lady! mooned Matt, gazing into Charming's melting dark eyes and recalling her extrovert performance in the bushes.

'Why didn't you tell me before about Charming?' asked Jenni with a puzzled frown. 'She sounds a super girl.'

Matt's chuckle echoed in the dimness of the passage. 'Ah didn't wanna go beatin' ma gums about Charmin'. Leastways, not while Ah thought there was a chance for you and me to have some fun! But Ah've come to realise,' he added slyly, 'you're a dame who prefers her doctors *very* experienced.'

Though her voice was cold with dignity, Jenni's inner response was electric. She clapped a hand against the fire in her chest. 'And what is that supposed to mean, Matthew Blamey?' Yes indeed, Matt Blamey, just what are you a-hinting at?

Chatting with an invisible Jenni

259

reduced to her skimpy underwear certainly loosened his tongue. He wanted her to be happy too. He wanted to share his happiness with the world. 'You and Dr Boss!' He raised his voice so she could hear better. 'Together you two would set the world on fire!'

'With our blazing rows, you mean,' Jenni snarled back, struggling to fasten the poppers on her white dress with fingers apparently made out of Play-doh. She found her hairbrush at the bottom of her rucksack and dragged the bristles viciously through her curly hair.

'Y'know what they say, Tadpole. Love and hate — opposite sides of the same coin,' chanted Matt, blithely unaware of the murderous sensations he was arousing in his unwilling listener. 'Yes, ma'am, Ah seen what was happening between you and Ross the Boss. When you came out here,' he rambled on amiably, 'Ah guessed it was on account of Big Poppa.'

Inside the stuffy little room Jenni choked for air. Her cheeks flamed red as poppies and her nails dug into the palms of her clenched fists. How dared Matt say such things!

But there was a greater shock to come. Matt hadn't finished yet.

'Course, you didn't know about him and Sylvia. Well, none of us did *officially*, though we had us our suspicions.'

Jenni collapsed on to the bench like a punctured balloon. Anger drained out of her, and in its place came a stunned sense of disbelief. What was this idiot telling her? *Paul* and Sylvia? Paul and *Sylvia*!

One of Matt's teases. It couldn't be.

She seemed to sit there for an age, her two hands clasped over her horrified mouth as, like a drowning swimmer with total recall, her inner vision replayed it all. Jenni raving on about Paul. Jenni reminiscing to a chilly Sylvia about the old times when he lived with the Westcott family at the vicarage. Jenni praising those husky bearded looks, the nobility of Paul's fine upstanding character, his dedication. No wonder Sylvia had looked sick as a parrot!

And idiot that I am, I meant so well, moaned Jenni, clutching her head in distress. I automatically assumed it was a doctor-nurse romance. Fancy matching poor Sylvia to the wrong partner . . . imagine the chaos if I ran a marriage bureau!

Matt thought he heard a faint groan. 'You OK in there?' He drummed his fingers on the green-painted wall. 'Need a hand with your buttons? . . . Did Ah tell you Ah seen Sylvia? She's over in the office cuddling up to Big Poppa and sobbin' her heart out over somethin' Ross told her. Ah don't know what, Tadpole. Maybe you can put me in the picture.'

Sister Bea's disembodied voice echoed in the corridor, interrupting this pleasant chat. 'Oh, there you are, Matt. Could you be a love and put up a drip for me? I'm short-handed, what with Sylvia running off like that.'

This galvanised Jenni. With one graceful movement she swept her hair into a ponytail and snapped an elastic band into place. Gone the dishevelled emotional girl, and in her place the calm professional woman.

Paul and Sylvia. They had concealed their feelings for each other so well. One never could have guessed.

She made haste for the children's ward to bury her sorrows in work.

# 9

Gradually Jenni came to realise that her distress stemmed from shock and did not truly reach heart-deep. She'd made a bit of a fool of herself — but heavens, it was only her pride that was suffering. She feared she must unwittingly have given Sylvia an uncomfortable time. Well, that was water under the bridge now, and when the couple announced their engagement she would pull all the stops out to show genuine delight.

Funnily enough, the prospect was quite heart-warming. For Jenni was discovering it wasn't just her pride putting a clown's mask on the face of tragedy. There was no tragedy. She genuinely did wish her friends a long and happy life together.

On her arrival at the Mbusa Wa Bwino Paul had quite literally swept her off her feet with shouts of delight at seeing 'his little Jenni' again after seven long years. But the reality wasn't a patch on the dreams. Oh yes, he was a hero of a man. But the chemistry wasn't there. For Paul's heart already belonged to Sylvia.

Jenni saw now how mistaken she'd been, assuming Paul never intended to marry. Sylvia and he had so much in common, had shared so many experiences together. It was right. It was good. It was meant to be. How delighted for him the Westcott family would be!

Jenni didn't say anything to Paul. As far as he and Sylvia knew, their secret was still theirs alone. They were unaware that Matt had been outside the office when a distraught Sylvia rushed past and abandoning her customary cool self-control hurled herself into Paul's arms. Thus had Matt put two and two together, passing his calculation on to a startled Jenni.

'Has Paul gone out?' she addressed her question to the only other person seated at the breakfast table.

She checked her watch. Ten past six. Tuesday. Funny . . . his truck was already gone. Surely he couldn't have forgotten she was taking out his stitches today? She glanced doubtfully at the scattering of crumbs and the small pile of dirty plates which testified to others having made an earlier start.

Jenni said with furrowed brow, 'I was supposed to take Paul's stitches out today.'

'I took them out myself,' returned the doctor crisply, noting the flicker of disappointment in her shadowy golden eyes. 'C'mon, have some toast. I don't think you eat enough. You look tired.' Maid Marian had lost her sparkle, and Ross shrewdly reckoned he knew why.

The nuns had taught the African cooks to bake their own bread. It quickly turned stale in a tropical climate, but made delicious toast for breakfast. Ross tipped two slices on to Jenni's clean plate. She stared at them for a moment, dully, as if lacking any appetite. Then she lifted her head and asked anxiously if the wound was satisfactory.

'Perfectly,' reassured the doctor, pulling his plate towards him and spreading margarine and marmalade thickly as if to help a listless child. 'Paul has taken Sylvia with him into Dar, just for a couple of days.' They had gone to buy an engagement ring, though Ross did not say so. On their return they planned a party for everyone: a farewell to Ross and an announcement of their own. The doctor had devised a scheme that would get Jenni herself away from the Mission and give the girl something concrete to worry about — like rampaging elephants and charging black rhino. With no one but Ross around to see, she'd have the chance to relax that stiff upper lip; and she could cry on his shoulder, if she chose to. Now was a good moment to broach his plan.

'When I officially finish my contract at the end of next week I plan to camp out for a few nights in one of the wildlife areas. How about you coming along to keep me company?' He didn't think he'd ever seen a face look more astonished! 'We could take a small tent, stay a couple of nights at Lake Manyara, travel on to the Serengeti National Park. It would do you the world of good to take a short break.'

'A break?' stuttered Jenni, completely thrown by the idea of spending a night in a small tent alone with Ross. So she'd been wrong about Sylvia: that couldn't alter the fact that there was a Mrs McDonnell somewhere back in the UK. And a nice girl didn't tangle with a married man. There led the road to ruin; all the agony aunties in the women's mags told you so.

Her eloquent hazel-gold eyes studied the harsh-lined unshaven face opposite hers. She looked down at her plate, and back up at Ross, forcing herself not to let his small rare kindnesses undermine her sense of what was right, and what would certainly be wrong! Literally trying to butter her up, wasn't he! Female companionship to while away the long dark nights. Well, he could jolly well look elsewhere. 'I can't imagine why *you* should be concerned,' she replied, protecting herself with cool sarcasm. 'I thought you'd have realised by now that my appearance is . . . deceptive. Anyway, there's too much to do here.'

Ross's grey eyes sparked with anger. She didn't fool him with her devotion to duty! 'If you don't want to come with me,' he said curtly, 'fair enough. Don't give it another thought.' Jenni raised her eyebrows and shrugged her slim shoulders, apparently very cool and uninterested. The rebuff was infuriatingly hurtful to Ross. His chair jerked backwards with a scrape of wood on uncarpeted floorboards. 'Remember this,' he snarled in a voice that sounded as if he'd gargled with diesel. 'I never ask a woman twice. So if you change your mind — send me a postcard!'

'*I never ask a woman twice,*'

mimicked Jenni as the doctor strode out, banging the doors behind him. Temper, temper! She really had got to him, hadn't she? He was the angry one now. And she was cucumber-cool. They seemed to have reversed their natures! she thought, rather excited that she could affect Ross so deeply. But she was in the right, she definitely was. He was cross as hell that she wasn't turning out as co-operative as the night when he'd taken her by surprise.

Deep down Jenni knew that through the long night hours she would be haunted by regrets. Oh, how she'd *love* a short break! To be totally alone with Ross on safari . . .

With a sigh she picked up the toast he'd buttered for her, bit into it with a crunch, smearing marmalade all over her chin. It was a wily invitation. He had reckoned on her being fully aware of what she was agreeing to — disguised as a break for her health and well-being! And Ross would have his fun without strings. Oh no, Dr

McDonnell, I've been around long enough to see that after the thrills comes the broken heart. And you could break my heart with your ruthless grey eyes alone.

But easier said than done. 'I never ask a woman twice!' he had promised grittily. And the finality of this preyed on Jenni's mind all through the morning.

By lunchtime she was feeling desperate and reckless. They might never meet again. Memories were all she would have, better memories than nothing! Yes, to get away for forty-eight hours or so would recharge her batteries, and she'd get to see the wild life of Tanzania in its natural habitat. She could always insist on *two* tents!

As the last mother and baby left the afternoon clinic, Jenni waited with beating heart for the right moment to approach Dr McDonnell and say to his face, as offhandedly as she could manage, right, I'll take you up on your invitation.

She was checking and filing record cards when Ross came in like a whirlwind, interrupting her busy thoughts, making her heart squeeze up like a concertina. Get a grip on yourself! warned Jenni's inner self. You want him to diagnose that you're suffering from fatal attraction?

But the doctor had weightier problems to deal with than Jenni's weak-kneed condition. Grim-faced, he strode over to the stone sink to wash his hands. 'Three cases of measles, and all from a settlement which hasn't yet had an inoculation programme.' Jenni saw the frown creasing his sun-burned forehead, her troubled eyes tracing the sensual furrows running from nose to mouth, more deep-etched by his sombre mood. 'I must get over there before the light goes, check all the children.'

Dusk fell around six and with great rapidity. 'I'm coming with you,' said Jenni in a don't-you-dare-refuse-me tone of voice, tents and safari parks quite forgotten. 'I'll pack a refrigerated bag with vaccines and antibiotics.' How many children were too sick for their mothers to struggle to the clinic for help? she wondered anxiously. The sore eyes, the rattling coughs, the skin rashes. Here in the bush, measles was a very different story from back home. These children were malnourished and physically weak. Pneumonia was a frequent complication. 'We could be facing an epidemic!'

'One shot of penicillin is a life-saver. I have to go.' Ross massaged his aching lower back. There'd been an obstetric emergency during the night. He'd give anything for a catnap! Crouching in window-less huts, dirty and rank with the smell of smoke, coaxing reluctant babies into the world — no picnic for someone of his height.

'Shan't be a minute,' said Jenni quickly, sensing a rare fatigue in the Boss. 'I'll tell Matt where we're going. Meet you in the dispensary in five minutes.'

She ran to her room and changed into jeans and a man-size T-shirt, grabbing a sweater as an after-thought. Ross drove on the close-shave side of dangerous along the dreadful roads with Jenni silent beside him, clinging on to the grab rail.

When they crunched down the last rutted track and pulled to a halt, it was clear that their forecast had been right and all was far from well.

'An evil spirit has come to our village and caused illness among our children,' mourned the people, flocking to meet them. Ross managed a rough translation which horrified Jenni.

'But why didn't they send for us sooner?' she agonised.

There was a dreadful wailing from a group of women and nurse and doctor were led into a hut where Jenni saw the saddest sight of her life. The medicine man had been unable to find the cause of the calamity and it was too late to save several small lives. She stumbled blindly from the hut and would have tripped had not Ross gripped her arm and wordlessly conveyed that she must steel herself to cope.

He estimated there were about twenty families in this small settlement. There was no time to be lost. One single shot of pencillin was often enough to clear up the lungs and save a child's life.

Ross indicated that he needed a small fire to boil water for sterilising hypodermic needles. The villagers set one burning with a slowness that had Jenni almost gibbering with impatience. Since there were no tables or chairs treatment had to be given there and then, crouching on the ground with the women kneeling on their haunches and the menfolk crowding round the group, their wailing forgotten as they watched nurse and doctor with absorbing curiosity.

Jenni never ceased to marvel at the African's stoical acceptance of pain. Mothers brought forward sad-looking children in slings on their backs, and offered their babes in arms. The people pressed closer to see the white man's medicine, and in particular the strange needle which those who had been to the clinic reported to have remarkable powers.

Ross didn't even bother to use his stethoscope on the moaning, coughing children. With the flat of his hand upon a burning chest he could feel the roughness of the breathing within.

Jenni held each child in her arms as it received its injection from the doctor. One tiny boy was coughing up the bloody froth indicative of pneumonia. 'Poor little things, they're so pitiful,' she whispered, forgetting no one but Ross could understand her. 'Why didn't they call us before? These are people who know we can help.'

'God knows!' Ross ground out bitterly. 'Feared more trouble from their spirits, I suppose. Here, get this lot sterilised for me. How are we off for penicillin?'

'We're doing OK. But what if Paul doesn't bring supplies back from Dar?

It's not as if this is his usual trip.'

'Then I'll have to drive there myself and pick up some more. That's the least of our problems. You can start worrying about how I get you back. I may be an expert with eyes, but even I have my limitations in the dark.'

He made it sound like a joke. Jenni wasn't seriously worried. As they rumbled away from the village she even managed a sneaking hope that they'd get well and truly lost and have to stop and crash out in the back of the Land Rover. One night alone with Ross. What a compromising situation! He'd have to marry her then — oh, hell's teeth, how could she have forgotten that he couldn't . . . Then to her everlasting shame she fell fast asleep and wasn't an ounce of help in getting them safely home. And it was Ross who staggered hollow-eyed to snatch a couple of hours' sleep and Jenni who was wide awake and full of regrets that after all she hadn't managed to tell him of her change of mind.

* * *

Everyone seemed to be doing disappearing acts these days. Paul and Sylvia had returned from Dar, but now the doctor had vanished and no one had seen him since the afternoon.

Paul had an announcement to make during supper. 'What will you have first?' he asked jovially. 'The good news — or the bad?'

Jenni sat there, puzzled. Paul couldn't be referring to his engagement, since Sylvia was openly sporting a modest diamond on the third finger of her left hand and the glad tidings were all round the Mission by now. Jenni had responded to the news with an enormous hug for the happy couple and a smacking kiss on Paul's bearded cheek. Ross had given her a very strange look, as if disapproving of her genuine delight. His attitude could be quite mystifying at times — but then, grimaced Jenni, he probably considered Paul would have done better to remain a bachelor!

She did rather hope Sylvia would never know about Helen, and it had been quite a shock when in the laundry room where they were rinsing out their white uniforms, Paul's new fiancée herself brought the matter up. 'Look, Jen,' she confided disarmingly, 'I wasn't very nice to you when you arrived, and I'm sorry about that. It was a misunderstanding. Paul has told me he was once engaged to your sister, and I've ticked him off for not telling me earlier. It must have been very awkward for you.'

On a surge of heady relief that such secrets were out in the open, Jenni decided now was the moment to clear her own conscience. 'Well, yes,' she admitted, 'but perhaps not quite in the way you mean. I — er — I thought you and Dr McDonnell were . . . I mean, I never realised about you and Paul, you see. I thought you might be going to marry Ross. Then I discovered he was married already,' she went on with a rush, 'and since no one else seemed to know about this I was desperately worried about whether I should tell you — or mind my own business!'

Hearing this, Sylvia had just shouted with laughter. 'Paul *and* Ross!' she hiccuped. 'Jen, I'm most flattered.' Then she sighed and her expression grew solemn. 'Ross's marriage,' she said darkly, tipping soapflakes into a bowl of warm water and adding several items of frilly peach underwear, 'is a tragedy. His wife is living openly with another man. I gather she's a very bright lady — lectures in French at the university near the hospital. Her boyfriend's in the same department and I suppose they inevitably saw a lot of each other. Good thing there's no children involved.'

'Must be dreadful for him, everyone knowing, no one to go home to at nights,' Jenni said unhappily, slipping her white dresses on to plastic hangers and hanging them up to drip dry.

'One night Ross stayed up late

talking to me and Paul. We'd opened one of those rare bottles of wine some kind soul sends out to us. He was tired and I dare say the wine loosened him up a bit. Paul told him about — well, about us. Ross was pleased, but it triggered off unhappy memories for him. He told us about Stefanie — so you see I did know about her. She's a Doctor — '

'A *doctor*? But I thought you said — '

'No, no — not a medical doctor. She's a D. Phil. Oxon. with an IQ you wouldn't believe. An academic, not a homemaker. She didn't want to cook or housekeep, and she told him she never wanted children. That shattered Ross. Well, they ended up living separate lives, even before she moved right out of their home and went off to live with this other guy.'

'Why didn't Ross get a divorce?' asked Jenni painfully.

Forgive me, Ross, for breaking your confidence, thought Sylvia. But better

Jen should know the truth instead of imagining you to be some sort of ogre. You married a bitch. You'll never say so.

'He saw the break-up of their marriage as his own failure — simple as that. Once he learns to love again, then he won't be able to end it quickly enough, mark my words.' Sylvia stared meaningfully at Jenni, willing her to remember all of this, not to forget one word.

'What do you think of these, Jen? Pure silk Janet Reger — well, I'd got a bit saved up and I thought, Sylvia, you only get married once in a lifetime . . .' She held up a dripping pair of lace-trimmed French knickers, seemingly unaware of the poignancy of what she had just said. In her case it would doubtless be true, brooded Jenni wistfully.

'Fancy you thinking that about me and Ross! You must have been daft.' Sylvia leaned against the windowsill and watched Jenni as she ironed. 'Paul and I — we've so much in common. It's crept up on us slowly. I mean, when I came out here I thought he was some kind of a monk, you know, with the nuns here and everything. Oh boy, do I know different now!'

Jenni was pressing collars and cuffs with far more care than usual, her troubled eyes glued to the hot iron.

'I admired Paul from afar but never allowed myself to think of him in — well, romantic terms,' reminisced the older nurse happily. 'Of course, Africa's in our blood now. I honestly don't think either of us could live anywhere else.' She thought for a moment or two and then said pointedly, 'It's going to take some getting used to, losing you and Ross. He's the sort of man who when he's not around you kind of . . . keep looking out for him, if you know what I mean.' Jenni nodded vaguely, giving nothing away, conscious of the other woman watching her very carefully. 'When you think of it, finding two highly gorgeous men in one small mission in the African bush is pretty extraordinary luck, Jen.'

Jenni looked Sylvia straight in the eye, unsmiling, saying nothing. One wasn't eligible. Surely Sylvia hadn't forgotten that?

Damn you, Ross, thought an exasperated Sylvia. I've done my best and got nowhere. Nothing encouraging to report. One last try. 'When you go back,' she asked boldly, 'will you keep in touch with Ross?'

'I don't suppose so. What would be the point? He won't be wanting to see me again.'

'I wouldn't be so sure,' came the cryptic reply.

*  *  *

With the tip of her finger Jenni pushed the little heap of spilled salt around the tablecloth. 'I'm sorry to tell you,' announced Paul, 'that our farewell-cum-engagement party planned for Saturday night will now have to be engagement only.'

284

Why? why? chorused the rows of stunned faces. 'Since our very good doctor has been spirited from our midst.' 'Oooh!' chorused the long table. 'The good news is that our new doctor arrives midday tomorrow. And our sad news is that we can't say a proper farewell to Ross and show our appreciation by giving him the bumps on Saturday night. Maybe he'll come back and visit us some day, who knows.'

'Why did he go?' demanded Jenni, her voice shrill with dismay. 'His contract runs till Friday.'

'Ross has been called home most urgently, to operate on a surgeon who's been injured in a car accident. This poor man asked for McDonnell and McDonnell alone — no one else would do. It's a case of saving the sight of another gifted man, and I'm sure you will all agree that Ross is on a top-priority mission, and our gratitude and our blessings go with him.'

★ ★ ★

Jenni spent her last night back at the Mission Headquarters in Dar-es-Salaam, in readiness for the late-morning flight. She slept in the very same room, reliving in sleepless longing that night when she had first set eyes on Ross McDonnell — looking like a cross between a demon and a tramp, she remembered with a delicious shiver. 'Taxi's here, wee Jenni,' called Sister Margaret. 'Have you got all your bags? Tch, this case weighs a ton, are you sure you can manage it on your own?'

'It's the souvenirs,' explained Jenni, 'for my parents and Helen and Hannah and their families.'

'Aye, of course. These two cases, please,' Sister told the driver. 'God bless you, child, and give you a safe journey home after your splendid work at the Good Shepherd. We don't want to lose you, but we know you must go, as the old song says. No, of course you won't know it, dear, much before your time. Are you quite sure you won't let anyone come to see you off?'

286

'I'll be fine,' promised Jenni, knowing that once she was in the anonymity of the airport she could wipe the stiff smile off her face and let her shoulders sag beneath the weight of unrequited love. At least in going home she would be on the same piece of terra firma as her beloved Ross.

She joined the queue to check her baggage in for the Heathrow flight and began the monotonous shuffle towards the brisk, uniformed girl at the desk. She had just arrived at the head of the queue and was about to hoist her first case on to the conveyor belt when a man's suntanned hand closed over hers and a voice said, 'Oh no, you don't!'

For a horrified moment Jenni thought she was being arrested for some unwitting Customs offence. But the navy sleeve reaching past her bore no official braid and there was something about the voice that was impossibly familiar.

'Miss Westcott will not be taking this flight,' she heard a man say. Her cases were swept off the ground and Jenni's stunned head tilted to take in the astonishing sight of Dr Ross McDonnell, immaculate and formal in a most elegant dark suit, with a crisp white shirt that emphasised he still had his tan and a *tie*, for goodness' sake!

He was walking off with her luggage and there wasn't much Jenni could do other than obediently troop after him.

Over by a pillar he set the cases down and turned to find her shaking with the hysterical tearful giggles she was trying to conceal behind her hands. 'Dear Ross! You're wearing a tie . . . Oh, Ross, you do look quite frighteningly handsome.' And indeed he did — her rough-diamond demon doctor transformed into the successful consultant which was his alter ego.

'*And* you've shaved,' she spluttered helplessly. 'Oh, Ross, what are you doing, what about my plane? Tell me what's going on!' She could hear her voice, blathering on, and there were tears on her cheeks and he'd whipped a spanking clean handkerchief from his breast pocket to wipe them away, putting his arms round her, lifting her off her feet so he could kiss her in front of everyone.

'I like your green dress. Haven't seen you in this before, have I? *Très chic* . . . Jennifer Westcott, I've spent the past twenty-four hours chasing round Africa after you!'

★ ★ ★

The lake teemed with freshwater life, dragonflies skimming its surface, the shore-lines patrolled by fishing birds, a small tent almost hidden among the frondy stems of papyrus. The air was full of bird sound and rippling water and the whirring of wings. English swallows were preening themselves under an African sun and a man and a woman were sharing a picnic right by the water's edge, yards from where gaudy gillimews with purple-red beaks were busily snatching small fish from the water.

'Perfect spot for a honeymoon,' said

Ross, 'but I'm afraid we may have to settle for the Caribbean instead.'

Within the circle of his arms Jenni twisted about to look up at him, her pretty face frowning at this disagreeable thought. 'Why can't we come back here?' she argued, nuzzling his neck and covering the side of his chin with pleading butterfly kisses.

He kissed the tip of her sun-speckled nose and silenced her mouth with another plump fresh date. 'Rainy season starts soon. There's already a tension in the air. Can't you feel it?'

'I feel nothing but the throb of your heartbeat,' she sighed, leaning back against her husband-to-be. 'But OK, Boss, Caribbean if you say so.' She sat up, momentarily distracted by goings-on among the lake's carpeting of waterlilies. 'Quick, pass the bird book. There's something nimbling about on the waterlily pads.'

'Nimbling,' chuckled Ross, stroking the line of her back through the flimsy cotton sundress. 'Dear Jenni, what sort of word is that? You're an original, you truly are. Those are sandpipers, my darling, searching for insects and other food, using the leaves for rafts. And those other greedy little chaps 'flailing the lily flowers to shreds as they dabble and deep-dive' are coots, according to page thirty-four. Coots is what they are, and what you've been, my lovely Jenni, resisting me for so long.'

'Don't you call me a coot, Dr McDonnell! I consider I've behaved with impeccable discretion.'

Ross groaned dramatically. 'Impeccable discretion! Is that what you call it? *I'd* describe it as the hard cold shoulder. Do you realise you could have lost me for good if it hadn't been for Sylvia writing me those fibs about you pining away with misery?'

'Hmm,' said Jenni, 'Nurse Anstey has hidden depths. I don't know how she could have dared. Besides, my resolve was definitely weakening. I'm a bad girl underneath and I'd have come looking for you in the end. You wouldn't have

escaped me for long, Ross McDonnell.'
She lay back on the rug they had laid
over the heat-baked grasses, flinging a
protective arm across her sun-dazzled
eyes, wondering how Dr Stefanie
McDonnell could have left so tender
and loving a man.

Reluctantly Ross had shown Jenni a
photograph of Stef taken at some
university do. It showed a tall fine-
boned blonde, in her early thirties and
extremely smartly dressed. It was
impossible to gauge anything of this
woman's character other than that she
was self-confident and sophisticated.
She certainly didn't look wicked or
wanton. In fact, thought Jenni uncomfortably, Stef was not unlike her own
sister Helen. She couldn't bring herself
to ask if Ross had shown this photo to
Paul.

*　*　*

When Ross had snatched Jenni from
the airport he had taken her to his hotel

and over a sumptuous lunch had asked her to listen to him very carefully. He had seen Stef. She could have the divorce she'd long been asking for. Jenni was never likely to have to meet her because Stefanie had dropped the bombshell that she and Trevor intended to leave the academic world, buy a vineyard and live permanently in rural France. Ross had shaken his head over this: a couple of totally impractical academics! Though he never wanted to see either of them again, he sincerely wished them well.

Stef had been very curious about Jenni, but Ross had refused to say anything more than that he was in love with a nurse he'd met in Africa. 'Good God,' Stef had exclaimed, 'you mean a black woman?'

Ross had sighed and said he wouldn't discuss the matter further.

Jenni almost choked on her noisettes of lamb. 'You told her you were going to marry again, when even *I* wasn't in on your plans?'

'Sylvia wrote and said you were breaking your heart missing me.'

'What a fib!'

'I know. She invented it, she told me so last night, but she was working on a hunch. Female intuition. Look me straight in the eye and tell me she was wrong . . . darling?'

An antelope sped by and Jenni and Ross turned to watch its graceful flight. Their heads swung from side to side in unison, there was so much to take in. 'See how each bird type fishes with its own idiosyncratic style,' pointed out Ross, drawing her gaze to the flamingoes with their crimson plumage and long sticklike legs; the black herons, their wings spread like Victorian parasols as they patrolled the shallows; a school of pelicans dipping their heads into the water like a formation team of swimmers.

'Ross,' sighed Jenni, 'what are we going to do?'

He hugged her close. 'Don't worry, sweetheart, I have it all worked out.

With your approval, this is what I sug-
gest. You'll be up for a Sister's post
when you get back. Yes? Well, you're
going to have to choose between me
and a Sister's frilly cap, because I'm
nearly thirty-eight and I want my wife
to start producing me a netball team — '

Jenni punched him playfully in the
ribs. 'Go on with you, don't you mean a
cricket team?'

'Netball team,' insisted Ross. 'I want
some little daughters with Titian plaits
and green hair ribbons.'

'And freckles?' she smiled tenderly.

'Freckles? Goes without saying.'

'You know how many's in a netball
team? You sure you can afford it?'

'Well, Sister Westcott, you'll be
wanting to get back to work as soon as
the youngest starts school, so we'll
manage somehow . . . If you care to
come to the tent I'll show you just what
I have in mind.'

'Oh, good thinking, Doctor! I was
wondering when you'd get round to
that.'

We do hope that you have enjoyed reading this large print book.

Did you know that all of our titles are available for purchase?

We publish a wide range of high quality large print books including:
**Romances, Mysteries, Classics**
**General Fiction**
**Non Fiction and Westerns**

Special interest titles available in large print are:
**The Little Oxford Dictionary**
**Music Book, Song Book**
**Hymn Book, Service Book**

Also available from us courtesy of Oxford University Press:
**Young Readers' Dictionary**
**(large print edition)**
**Young Readers' Thesaurus**
**(large print edition)**

For further information or a free brochure, please contact us at:
**Ulverscroft Large Print Books Ltd.,**
**The Green, Bradgate Road, Anstey,**
**Leicester, LE7 7FU, England.**
**Tel:** (00 44) 0116 236 4325
**Fax:** (00 44) 0116 234 0205

*Other titles in the*
*Linford Romance Library:*

## SINISTER ISLE OF LOVE

### Phyllis Mallett

Jenny Carr is joining her brother on the Caribbean island of Taminga to start a new life. On her way, she meets Peter Blaine, a successful businessman on the island. He couldn't be more of a contrast to Craig Hannant, whose business is failing. His wife had died in mysterious circumstances, and Craig is now a difficult man to be around — but Jenny falls for Craig, despite all the signs that she is making the biggest mistake of her life . . .

# CUPID'S BOW

## Toni Anders

When romantic novelist Janey first meets Ashe Corby, she is not impressed. But frustratingly, the hero in the latest novel she is writing persists in resembling him! As Janey gets to know Ashe, she comes to admire and like him. But when she attempts to help Ashe's son Daniel to realise his dream of studying horticulture, Ashe is furious at what he sees as interference on Janey's part. Miserable without each other, will love win through for them?